The Finding of the Grail

RETOLD FROM OLD FRENCH SOURCES

∾

Patricia Terry and Nancy Vine Durling

University Press of Florida

GAINESVILLE · TALLAHASSEE · TAMPA · BOCA RATON

PENSACOLA · ORLANDO · MIAMI · JACKSONVILLE · FT. MYERS

Copyright 2000 by the Board of Regents of the State of Florida
Printed in the United States of America on acid-free paper
All rights reserved

05 04 03 02 01 00 6 5 4 3 2 1

LIBRARY OF CONGRESS CATALOGING-IN-PUBLICATION DATA
Terry, Patricia Ann, 1929–.
The finding of the Grail: retold from Old French sources /
Patricia Terry and Nancy Vine Durling.
p. cm.
Includes bibliographical references.
ISBN 0-8130-1788-2 (alk. paper) 0-8130-2488-9 (pbk)
1. Perceval (Legendary character) — Romances — Adaptations.
2. Chrétien de Troyes, 12th cent. — Adaptations. 3. Grail — Romances —
Adaptations. I. Durling, Nancy Vine, 1953– . II. Title.
PS3570.E729 F55 2000
841'.1–dc21   00-023446

The University Press of Florida is the scholarly publishing agency for the
State University System of Florida, comprising Florida A&M University,
Florida Atlantic University, Florida Gulf Coast University, Florida
International University, Florida State University, University of Central
Florida, University of Florida, University of North Florida, University
of South Florida, and University of West Florida.

University Press of Florida
15 Northwest 15th Street
Gainesville, FL 32611-2079
http://www.upf.com

CONTENTS

~

FIGURES

Illustrations were taken from the following thirteenth- and fourteenth-century French manuscripts and are reproduced here with the kind permission of the Bibliothèque Nationale in Paris. Some of them (from manuscripts 1453, 12577) are from Chrétien de Troyes's *Conte du graal* and the Continuations; others are from different grail narratives (contained in manuscripts 95, 110, 344, 24394) or from unrelated manuscripts with scenes similar to those recounted in the grail stories.

(BN ff = Bibliothèque Nationale, Paris, fonds français)

BN ffr 1453 (fourteenth century): contains Chrétien de Troyes's *Perceval*, First Continuation, Second Continuation, Manessier.

BN ffr 12577 (fourteenth century): contains Chrétien de Troyes's *Perceval*, First Continuation, Second Continuation, Manessier.

BN ffr 95 (thirteenth century): contains Robert de Boron's *L'Estoire del saint graal*, *L'estoire de Merlin* (f. 113), *Le Roman des Sept Sages de Rome* (in prose [f. 355]), *La Penitence Adam* (f. 380).

BN ffr 110 (thirteenth century): contains Robert de Boron's *L'Estoire del Saint Graal*, *L'Estoire de Merlin* (f. 45), *Le Roumans de Lancelot del Lac* (*La Quête du Saint Graal* and *La Mort d'Arthus de Gautier Map* [f. 163]).

BN ffr 24394 (fourteenth century): contains Robert de Boron's *L'Estoire del saint graal*.

BN ffr 334 (fourteenth century): contains *Le Roman de Tristan* (in prose).

BN ffr 749 (thirteenth century): contains Robert de Boron's *Le Roman du Saint Graal*, *L'Estoire de Merlin* (f. 122v).

BN ffr 770 (thirteenth century): contains Robert de Boron's *Le Roman du Saint Graal*, *Li Romans de Merlin* (f. 122), *Histoire de la prise de Jérusalem* (f. 313).

ACKNOWLEDGMENTS

Many friends and colleagues have been kind enough to read drafts of this project and we have benefited greatly from their suggestions. We are especially grateful to Elena Aguilar, Renate Blumenfeld-Kosinski, Maureen Boulton, Matilda Bruckner, Mason Cooley, Renée Geen, Kathleen Micklow, and Susan Smith for their helpful comments.

Jeanette Beer provided a welcome opportunity to discuss the project in a session devoted to the translation of medieval texts at the Thirty-first International Congress on Medieval Studies at Kalamazoo, Michigan, in 1996.

We wish to thank University Press of Florida readers Regina Psaki and Christopher Callahan, who helped us make a number of final adjustments and changes that significantly improved the text.

Our very special thanks go to Robert M. Durling and Robert Terry, who encouraged this enterprise at every stage and made valuable suggestions.

INTRODUCTION

The phrases "King Arthur," "Round Table," and "Holy Grail" will be
familiar to any reader of this book; they may well be found in today's
newspaper. The images they evoke seem part of an ageless myth, although
the legendary king and his court may originally have had a basis in histori-
cal fact. Several early medieval chronicles refer to a fifth-century British
chieftain named Arthur who successfully, though briefly, defended the
Celts against the Anglo-Saxons.[1] In the early twelfth century, Geoffrey of
Monmouth transformed this warrior into a great king whose conquests
would have included even Rome had it not been for the tragic ending of his
story. Geoffrey's fanciful *History of the Kings of Britain* (ca. 1130) brings
into literature many elements of the Arthurian court as we know it today:
the king's nephew Gawain, Kay the seneschal, Guenevere, Mordred, a
court refined by the presence of noble ladies.[2] Geoffrey was Welsh; his
work was written in Latin prose, and in conformity with the taste of the
Norman rulers of England.

Across the Channel and slightly later, another vision of Arthur was
developing in the romances of the French poet Chrétien de Troyes.[3] In
these stories, the king is a secondary figure and the adventures belong to
heroic knights of the Round Table. These lone knights ride through trackless forests, testing their courage against whatever comes. Their presence
means danger for oppressors and hope for the oppressed. Knights errant
will enter mysterious realms where fountains generate storms, lances may
burst into flame or bleed, castles appear and disappear—these elements of
Celtic mythology give the Arthurian romances their fairy-tale quality. And
always, in the course of their adventures, the knights will fall in love.

Little is known of Chrétien de Troyes who, judging from information
gleaned from the prologues to his works, seems to have been active be-

tween 1160 and 1180, first in Champagne at the court of the countess Marie (daughter of Eleanor of Aquitaine), and later in Flanders. All of Chrétien's surviving works are written in French and are composed in octosyllabic couplets. His first four romances, *Erec and Enide*, *Cligès*, *Yvain, or the Knight of the Lion*, and *Lancelot, or the Knight of the Cart*, are all approximately 7,000 lines long and celebrate the adventures of individual knights who struggle to achieve a balance between love and valor. *Perceval, or the Story of the Grail* is Chrétien's last major work and is dedicated to a new patron, Philippe d'Alsace, count of Flanders (d. 1191). This 9,234-line work marks a new departure in both content and structure. Although unfinished, *Perceval* is considerably longer than the earlier romances; in it the Holy Grail appears for the first time. While it is true that Chrétien develops, particularly in *Yvain*, the idea that a knight's true glory lies in service to others, in *Perceval* this conception of chivalry is expanded to include a broader range of spiritual concerns.

The Story of the Grail is essentially a story of education: a youth, Perceval, who is raised in ignorance of his aristocratic heritage, aspires to knighthood. He soon learns the skills of a warrior and practices them in the world to great effect, but loses, in the process, his childlike simplicity. This evolution is not easy to evaluate. Education and experience, in the domain of love, achieve the transformation of a brutish fellow, completely lacking in feeling for others, into the refined lover of the elegant lady Blanchefleur. But in the domain of the grail, his education causes Perceval to suppress his natural curiosity and thus to fail. After his initial encounter with the grail in the castle of the Fisher King, Perceval returns to Arthur's court, where the assembled knights are invited to undertake a number of possible adventures. Gawain, often portrayed as the embodiment of courtly charm and knightly valor, elects to attempt the rescue of the Lady of Montesclaire. Perceval rejects all such worthy but conventional challenges and, in Chrétien's words, *redist tot el*, speaks quite otherwise, vowing never to rest until he once again sees the grail. At first his quest continues in the usual modes of knight errantry, and although Perceval is reoriented by a hermit, we do not know whether Chrétien would have allowed him ultimate success. At just this point in the story, Perceval disappears, and the narrative turns to the adventures of Gawain, later breaking off without a conclusion.

Thirteenth-century readers were eager to know more about the exploits of these two knights, and verse continuations of Chrétien's romance soon began to appear. Our own twenty-first-century prose version continues this medieval tradition of retelling and expanding the tale. We have selected episodes from these earliest continuations and woven them together into a complete story.[4] Our procedure was inspired not only by the continuators, but by Chrétien himself, who—if we may judge by his statement in the prologue to his first romance, *Erec and Enide*—took pride in his ability to combine disparate materials into a seamless whole. Here the author tells us that the episodes comprising the romance have been bound together through a *molt bele conjointure,* a meaningful conjoining, or unity. We have been guided in our choices by respect for Chrétien's balanced view of human aspirations and his delicate irony, which excludes narrow, intolerant views, religious or otherwise. Perhaps the greatest of his gifts was the ability to combine, in a mutually enhancing way, the mysterious and the mundane. It is this celebration of life in all its variety that we have sought to convey in our retelling of his tale.

NOTES

1. For discussion of the early chronicle tradition, see Robert W. Hanning, *The Vision of History in Early Britain: From Gildas to Geoffrey of Monmouth* (New York: Columbia University Press, 1966).

2. For an English translation, see *History of the Kings of Britain*, translated by Sebastian Evans, revised by Charles W. Dunn (New York: E. P. Dutton, 1958).

3. Chrétien may also have drawn inspiration from the verse "retelling" of Geoffrey of Monmouth by the Norman court poet Wace, whose *Roman de Brut* (ca. 1155) includes a long section about Arthur and introduces the Round Table. Jean Frappier's *Chrétien de Troyes: The Man and His Work*, translated by Raymond J. Cormier (Athens: Ohio University Press, 1982) provides a good introduction to Chrétien's romances.

4. Our choice of materials and our methods are discussed in the afterword.

The Finding of the Grail

RETOLD FROM OLD FRENCH SOURCES

~

I
T WAS THE TIME OF YEAR when trees once again unfurl new leaves, and the meadow grass and woods begin to turn green; mornings resound with the sweet language of birds, and every living thing is alight with joy. In the solitude of the Deserted Forest, the widow's son awoke. He rose quickly, saddled his horse and, taking three javelins, went out of his mother's house. He thought he would go watch the laborers sowing grain, with a pair of oxen for each of their six harrows. He started into the forest, but the beauty of the day and the birds' joyful music made him so happy that he took off his horse's bridle and let him graze where he would in the fresh grass. Meanwhile the boy amused himself with his javelins, casting them with great skill, backwards and forwards, up and down.

A commotion interrupted the peaceful morning as five knights, fully armed, came riding through the woods. The boy heard the crack of branches snapped off oak and ironwood trees, the shock of spear against shield, chain mail, wood and metal crashing together. He caught only a glimpse of the knights, but he suddenly thought of the devils his mother had warned him about. She said they were the ugliest things in the world, and you had to make the sign of the Cross if you saw one. That he disdained to do because "my javelin will take the biggest of them, and the others will stay away."

But as the knights came closer, he saw them more clearly. The light glinted on their armor, sparkled on their tall helmets; white and vermilion, gold, azure, and silver shone in the sunlight. Struck with wonder, the boy thought, "I was wrong to call them devils—they are angels! Mother told me that angels are the most beautiful things in the world, except for God. And that one, the most beautiful of all, must surely be God himself!" He threw himself down on the ground and began to recite the prayers his mother had taught him.

The leader of the knights exclaimed, "Stay back! There's a boy over here. He must have been terribly frightened, so let's not all go over to him at once. I want to ask him some questions." The others stopped while their leader rode up to the boy and greeted him kindly, saying, "Don't be afraid."

"Of course not! Aren't you God?"

"No!"

"Then who are you?"

"I am a knight."

"I have never met a knight, and I've never even heard of one before, but you must be as beautiful as God. I wish I were made of silver like you!"

The knight rode up close to him. "Did you see five men and three maidens crossing this heath today?"

But the boy had other thoughts in mind and other questions to ask. Putting his hand on the knight's lance, he said, "My lord, you who are called a knight, tell me what this is."

"Things have taken a strange turn," said the knight. "I thought, my young friend, to learn something from you, but instead you would learn from me. So be it. That is my lance."

"Do you throw it the way I do my javelins?"

"Of course not! You use it to strike mighty blows."

"Then I'd rather have my javelins. I can throw them as far as an arrow can fly, and kill all the birds and animals I want to."

"Perhaps, but we're not interested in that. Tell us, boy, have you seen the knights and the maidens? Do you know where they are now?"

But the boy put his hand on the shield. "What do you call this," he asked, "and what is it for?"

"That isn't fair! I thought you would answer my question, not ask me another! But I will tell you anyway. That is called a shield."

"A shield?"

"Yes, and it must be treated with respect. It is such a faithful friend that it stands between me and a blow from lance or arrow."

The others now came forward, wanting to know what "the Welsh fellow" was saying.

"He has no idea how to behave," the knight replied. "No matter what I ask him he won't give a straight answer, but asks instead what something of mine is called and how it is used."

"You are wasting time, my lord. Everyone knows the stupidity of the Welsh. You might as well question an ox in a pasture!"

"Nevertheless, I've a mind to answer his questions, and do not intend to leave before I have done so." He turned to the boy again:

"Just tell me whether you saw the knights and maidens!"

But the boy had a grip on the chain mail of his hauberk. "Sir knight, what is this?"

"Don't you know?"

The boy shook his head.

"This is a hauberk. They are made of iron."

"I have never heard of such a thing, but it's beautiful. What do you use it for?"

"That's easy to say. If you hit me with a javelin or an arrow, you will do me no harm."

"Then may God keep the deer and stags from wearing such hauberks! They would be safe from me forever."

The knight tried once again. "As you hope for salvation, young fellow, tell me what you know of the knights and maidens."

The boy, obtuse as he was, replied, "Were you born that way?"

"Of course not! No one is born in armor!"

"Who gave it to you, then?"

"All this equipment was given to me by King Arthur, less than five years ago when he dubbed me a knight. But now answer my question. Did the five knights and the maidens seem to be in a hurry?"

"My lord, look where the trees are tallest, high on the mountain. That is the Valbone Pass."

"What about it?"

"My mother's people are working up there. If anyone went that way, they will tell you."

The knight asked the boy to be their guide.

When the laborers saw him riding toward them, they were terrified. They knew how his mother had tried to keep him away from knights. Now he would want to be one, and she would go mad with grief. He asked them if they had seen five men and three maidens.

"Yes, and they can't have gone far."

The boy turned to the knights' leader. "My lord, they went this way! But now tell me again about the king who makes knights, and where he can be found."

"I saw the king not five days ago at Carduel. If he is not there, someone will surely tell you where to look next."

The knights galloped away, and the youth hurried home. His mother, nearly frantic, ran to meet him, exclaiming, "I have been so worried! Where were you?"

"Mother! I've seen something so wonderful! There were men riding through the forest, more beautiful than anything in the world."

She put her arms around him and said: "May God protect you! They must have been evil spirits!"

"No, no, Mother! They said they were knights!"

On hearing the word "knights" his mother fainted. When she came to, she began to weep. "Listen to me, my child. You would have been a knight yourself, had it pleased God to watch over your father and his friends. Your father was the bravest man in the world. And my own father was a great knight too. But these are terrible times. Valor accomplishes nothing—it only leads to death. Your father was wounded in battle; his whole body sickened, and he could not fight any more. When King Uther Pendragon died, your father's lands, his wealth, everything he had was lost. We were forced to flee and brought your father to the one place left to him, here in the Deserted Forest. When you were still very young, your two brothers were sent to be trained as knights. The older went to the king of Escavalon, the other to Ban of Gomorret. Years later they were knighted on the same day and set out for home. But we never saw them again. They were found dead by the side of the road, their eyes plucked out by crows. Your father died of grief when he heard the news, and I have lived in bitterness ever since. You were my one comfort, my one consolation, all God left me of happiness and joy."

But the boy was paying no attention. "I'm hungry," he said. "Please give me something to eat. I want to go see that king who makes knights!"

Nothing his mother said could dissuade the boy. In the end, she made him some sturdy clothes of burlap and leather, and three days later he left. Her last words to him were, "I wish you would not go, but if you must, remember these things: Ask the king himself for arms. You won't know how to use them, but you will learn by watching others. Always honor and protect women. If you win a kiss from a woman you are fortunate indeed, but you must not take more. If she gives you a ring or a gift, you may accept it. Be sure to ask the name of anyone you travel with. Keep company only with honorable men. Above all, go to church and say your prayers."

"What is a church?"

"People go there to pray, and—"

But the boy would hear no more. He saddled his horse and mounted.

"God go with you, my son," his mother said. "May he give you all the joy I am losing forever!" A stone's throw away, he looked back and saw her lying on the ground as if she were dead. He struck his horse with a stick, and galloped away. All day long he rode and never stopped; that night he slept in the forest.

Early the next morning he set out again and soon found himself in a broad meadow with a brook running through it. There he saw a beautiful tent, with panels of crimson and gold. On top, a gilded eagle sparkled in the sun. Entranced, the boy dismounted and walked right in. A maiden, sound asleep, lay on a bed draped in silk.

As he stood staring at her, his horse gave a loud whinny, and the girl sprang to her feet. She was terrified. What a fool she had been to stay there all alone!

"Get out!" she cried.

"But I want to kiss you!"

"Never! Go away before my lover comes back! If he finds you here, he will kill you!"

But the young man was undeterred; with his powerful arms, he caught her in an embrace. Despite her protests and attempts to break free, he held her tight, and covered her face with kisses. Then he saw an emerald ring on her finger.

"My mother told me that I could take a ring, but nothing more."

"You'll never have it! Never!"

Grabbing her clenched fist, the youth pried open her fingers and took the ring, placing it on his own finger. She wept and pleaded: "Please don't take my ring! My lover will never believe me, and sooner or later you'll pay for it with your life."

The boy ignored her and turned to leave. On his way out, he spied a small barrel of wine with a silver goblet next to it, and under a clean white cloth were three goatmeat pies—a welcome sight! He poured some wine and gulped it thirstily. Then he seized one of the pies. "These shouldn't go to waste! Come have some—they look good!"

He ate his fill and took his leave, saying: "Thank you, lovely lady. And don't worry about the ring. I can take care of myself!" The trembling girl made no reply but just kept weeping.

Very soon her lover returned from the woods and was surprised to see fresh hoofprints leading away from the tent. "Lady, you have had a visitor."

"No, my lord, it was just a young Welsh boy—a stupid, rustic fellow, who helped himself to your wine and pies."

"Then why are you crying? Why would I care about that?"

"There's something else, my lord. He stole my ring."

The knight began to feel uneasy. "This is an outrage! But as long as you are all right, it doesn't matter."

"My lord, he kissed me."

"Kissed you?"

"I tried to stop him, but he was too strong. There was nothing I could do."

"And you liked it, didn't you?"

Tormented by jealousy, he went on: "I have always known you were faithless! But you'll regret this! We're leaving right now and we won't stop until I have cut your lover's head from his shoulders. If your horse dies, you can follow me on foot, in the clothes you have on now."

Meanwhile the boy went his way, until he saw a coal merchant driving a donkey. "Sir," he said, "is this the road to Carduel? I want to see King Arthur who makes knights."

"Just keep going. You'll find him in a castle by the sea, and he will be both happy and sad."

"What do you mean?"

"King Arthur and his knights have just defeated King Rion—that's why Arthur is happy. But now all the lords are going back to their lands, and so he is sad."

The boy thought this was a strange way to talk, but he rode on, and soon the splendid castle was before him. A knight in bright red armor galloped out through the gate. In one hand he held the reins, in the other a golden goblet. Overcome with envy, the boy thought, "I want that armor!" As he started toward the castle, the knight called out to him, "Where do you think you're going?"

"I'm going to ask the king if I can have your armor."

"You do that! I'll wait for you right here. And while you are at it, tell the king that if he doesn't want to yield his land to me, he had better send someone to fight for it. I am its rightful lord. Just look at this goblet! I took it right out of the king's hand!"

But this did not interest the boy, who couldn't wait to get to court. He rode his horse right into the great square hall where many angry-looking knights were gathered. The boy asked one of them to point out the king, then pushed his way through the crowd to the high table. With an awkward bow, he spoke as courteously as he could but received no reply. He tried again, and again the king was silent. "How can this be the king who makes knights?" he wondered. "He doesn't even talk!" He was just about to leave, when Arthur raised his head and greeted him kindly.

"Welcome to my court. Forgive my silence, I was too angry to speak! The Red Knight was just here contesting my land—he's crazy enough to believe it is rightly his. I would not have cared about that, but he snatched away my goblet, spilling wine all over the queen. She felt so humiliated that she has locked herself in her rooms. We haven't decided how best to avenge the insult."

The boy's eyes were bright and laughing; he cared nothing about the king's troubles. "Make me a knight right now, Sir King! I want to be on my way."

"My friend," said the king, "dismount and let a servant take your horse. I will make you a knight soon enough."

"Please do it right now so I can leave. Let me have the armor of that knight I saw outside—the one who took the goblet."

The seneschal Kay, annoyed by the boy's presumption, said, "You are right, my friend! Go take his armor. It's yours!"

Kay's joke at the boy's expense angered the king. "You are unkind, Sir Kay! If the boy doesn't know any better, it's not his fault. By his appearance, he is of noble birth. He could be a worthy knight one day, but not if he throws his life away for nothing."

While the king was speaking to Kay, a lovely maiden approached the boy and looked up at his open, eager face. Laughing, she said to him, "If you live long enough, young man, you will be the greatest knight the world has ever seen."

This maiden had not laughed for more than six years, and everyone was astonished. Kay jumped up and slapped her so hard she fell to the ground. Then he saw Arthur's jester, standing near the fireplace, and kicked him so that he stumbled into the flames. This was because the jester had often said, "That maiden will laugh when she sees the greatest knight in the world."

The boy, however, was impatient to be off. Yvonet wanted to find out what would happen, so he slipped away and took a shortcut to a place from which he could see the Red Knight. He had put the golden goblet on a rock and was looking about impatiently. The boy rode right up to him, shouting, "Give me your armor! King Arthur says I can have it!"

"You again! Tell me, is no one coming to defend the king's honor?"

"That is *my* armor! Take it off right now!"

"Pay attention, boy! I am asking you who is coming to fight me."

"Knight, if you don't hurry up, I'll hit you!"

The knight's response was to take his lance in both hands and flatten the boy against the neck of his horse. Furious and in pain, he sprang up and hurled his javelin straight through the Red Knight's eye, spattering his face with blood and brains. Then he jumped off his horse and stared at his dead opponent. He took the knight's lance and removed the shield from around his neck, but he could not get the helmet off, nor could he pull the sword from its scabbard. Yvonet, smiling, came up to him and said, "What are you trying to do?"

"The king gave me this armor, but how do I get it off the knight? You can't tell where he ends and it begins."

"I can remove it, if you like," said Yvonet.

"Yes, please!"

Yvonet set to work, and soon the knight was disarmed from head to toe. Hauberk, greaves, helmet, and all the rest of the armor lay on the ground. Yvonet urged the boy to put on the padded silk garments the knight wore underneath, but he answered, "Are you joking? Why would I exchange these good clothes my mother made for that thin stuff? It wouldn't even keep the water off!"

He would take nothing but the armor. Yvonet helped him put on the hauberk, greaves, and helmet, girded on his sword, and fastened the spurs over his rough leather shoes. The boy said, "Friend, take my horse if you like. He's a good one, but I like this one better. Give the goblet to the king, and greet him for me. And tell the girl that if I can, I will make Kay sorry he slapped her." With that they parted.

Yvonet went straight to court and gave the king his goblet, "with the good wishes of the knight who was just here."

"You mean the Welsh boy who asked for the Red Knight's armor?"

"Yes."

"How did he get my goblet? Did the Red Knight make him a gift of it?"

"Quite the reverse. The boy had to kill him."

"What?"

"The knight struck him with his lance. Then the boy flung his javelin straight through his eye. And Sire, the boy asked me to tell the maiden Kay struck down that he will avenge her if he can."

The jester, overjoyed, ran to the king: "Sire, this is the first of many great and wonderful adventures. The day will come when the young knight will make Kay regret what he did. His right arm will be broken above the elbow—he will wear it in a sling for half a year."

Kay was so outraged that he wanted the jester to be killed, but he knew Arthur would never permit it.

The king said, "Kay, if you had not misled that boy, he could have been taught to use shield and lance and no doubt would have made a fine knight. As things are, he does not even know how to draw his sword. He is out there riding around in his armor, and anyone who wants a fine horse has only to attack him. He will surely be maimed or killed." But the king's reproaches changed nothing.

*   *   *

THE BOY WENT RIDING through the forest and then across a plain until he came to a river so dark and deep he dared not cross. As he rode along the bank gazing at the high cliffs on the other side, he became aware of castle walls that seemed to rise straight out of the rock. There were four round towers; a taller one stood in their midst. Leading to the castle was a stone bridge, part of which could be raised, and as the boy rode toward it, he saw a gentleman in a dark purple cloak strolling along. He held a slender staff, as befitted his rank, and was accompanied by two squires. The boy, remembering his mother's instructions, greeted the nobleman politely.

"God be with you," he replied, seeing that the boy was very young and all alone. "Where did you come from today?"

"From King Arthur's court."

"And what were you doing there?"

"The king made me a knight."

"A knight! I thought he was too busy these days to make any knights. Tell me, who gave you that armor?"

"The king."

"Did he indeed?"

And the boy told the whole story. Afterwards the nobleman asked him how he liked riding a warhorse.

"He goes even better than my old one!"

"And how does that armor feel?"

"It's so light I hardly know I have it on."

"Good! Tell me, if you will, what brings you here?"

"My mother taught me to seek out worthy men wherever I might find them, and heed their advice."

"God bless your mother—she is very wise."

"Do you think I could stay here tonight?"

"Certainly. But first you have to promise me something. You will not regret it!"

"What?"

"To follow your mother's advice, and mine as well."

"I promise."

"Then dismount."

And so he did. One of the servants took his horse, and the other removed his armor. There he stood in his ill-fitting deerskin tunic and crudely made shoes.

Wearing the boy's sharp spurs, the nobleman mounted his horse, hung the shield around his neck, and grasped the lance. "Now, my friend, I'll show you something about jousting." He demonstrated how the shield should be held—a little forward and against the neck of the horse. Couching the lance and holding it against the saddle guard, he spurred the magnificent horse, which responded with tremendous speed. The nobleman had learned all this in his youth and was truly accomplished. At the end of the demonstration, he raised his lance and reined up beside the delighted boy, who said that he did not want to live another day without being able to ride like that. "If you put in the effort, you will learn. Anything worth doing requires practice and dedication. It is not your fault if you have never had a chance to try it before."

But when the nobleman invited him to mount, the boy rode as if he had spent his whole life in tournaments and wars. He was born for this, and when nature and inclination combine, nothing is difficult. Reining up with his lance raised, as he had seen the older man do, he asked, "My lord, how was that? Do you think I could really learn? I've never in my life wanted anything so much! Please will you teach me all you know?"

"If you truly wish it."

And so the nobleman began to teach him. He would demonstrate a maneuver and then have the boy mount and do it himself. After the third time, he asked, "My friend, if you met a knight and he struck you, what would you do?"

"I would strike him back."

"And if your lance broke?"

"Then I would fight him with my fists."

"No, you would not."

"What then?"

"Challenge him with your sword."

"I would rather use my javelin. I used to practice all the time at my mother's, and I can hit anything."

"We'll talk about that later, but now let's go back to the house."

They walked along, side by side, and presently the boy said to his host, "Sir, my mother told me that I should never be long in someone's company without asking his name. What is yours?"

"I am Gornemant of Gorhaut."

As they were going up the steps to the fine large house, a servant came running with a short cloak for the boy, so that he would not take cold after his exertions. Their dinner was all prepared, and as soon as they had washed, they sat down to eat. Gornemant had the boy sit beside him. I will not tell you about all the dishes they had or what they drank, but you can be sure it was all delicious. The nobleman invited the boy to stay with him for a month, or a whole year, if he wished. He would teach him everything he needed to know. The boy replied, "Sir, I don't know if my mother's house is nearby, but I pray that God will let me see her again. When I left, she was so upset she fell in a faint. I don't even know if she is dead or alive. That is why I can't stay. I must leave tomorrow."

Gornemant saw that he would not change his mind, and soon they retired for the night. In the morning, the nobleman went to where the boy was sleeping and had the servants bring a fine shirt, russet leggings, and a tunic of purple silk from India. As his gifts were carried in, he said, "My friend, I hope you will dress in these clothes."

"Why do you want me to? Mine are better."

"Believe me, they are not."

"I think they are."

"Remember, you promised to do everything I asked."

The boy considered. "That is true," he at last replied. "I will do as you say." And he put on the new clothes.

The knight knelt down and fastened on the boy's right spur, as was the custom when a new knight was created. Squires hastened to help with his armor. Gornemant girded on his sword, embraced him, and said, "You now belong to the order of chivalry, which must be without stain. It is the highest order established by God, and there are certain things you must remember. First, if you defeat a knight and he asks for mercy, always grant it. Second, do not be too talkative. The longer the speech, the greater the fool. Third, do all you can to help orphans and women in need. Finally, go often to church, and pray the Creator to have mercy on your soul and protect you in this life."

"That is just what my mother told me!"

"But you must promise me one thing more. Stop saying your mother taught you about such things. It makes you sound like a fool."

"What should I say?"

"Say that the knight who strapped on your spur taught you."

When he had promised always to say that Gornemant was his teacher, the older man raised his hand in blessing: "Go with God, and may He protect you."

The new knight rode away. Several days had passed since he left his home, and he was eager to see his mother again. He took the path through the deep forest, more familiar to him than open plains. Then, across bare, desolate lands he saw a great castle at the very edge of the sea. To reach the entrance he would have to go over a bridge so dilapidated it might not bear his weight. He managed to cross safely, but the gate on the other side had been shut fast. He beat on it with his fists, calling out at the top of his voice, until a thin, pale maiden looked out of a window and said, "Who is there?"

"A knight who hopes to find shelter."

"My lord," she replied, "you shall have it, but I'm afraid it may not be to your liking. We will try to make you as comfortable as we can." With that she disappeared.

Nothing happened. He had just begun to shout again when four armed servants appeared, battle-axes in their hands and swords at their sides. Together they unlocked the heavy gate and swung it open, inviting the knight to come in. They would have been handsome men, had fasting and watchfulness not taken their toll.

The knight was shocked by what he found inside. If the surrounding lands were desolate, no less so were the streets and houses within the castle walls. There was no one in sight. Two big churches had fallen to ruin; the houses, also, were in sad disrepair, roofless, and at the mercy of the elements. Mills stood motionless. No fires had been lit for the preparation of food. There was nothing for sale, no wine, no bread. All was silent.

The four men led him toward a fine dwelling with a slate roof; here he dismounted and was relieved of his armor. A young squire came down the steps, carrying a light gray cloak which he placed around the knight's shoulders. Another youth stabled the horse, though there was little to offer him of hay or oats. Meanwhile, the knight was escorted up the stairs and into the great hall, where two men and a maiden came to greet him. The men were of powerful build, their hair tinged with silver, but not yet white; had they not endured so much suffering, they would have seemed in the prime of life. As for the young woman, she was as elegant and graceful as a sparrow hawk, as colorfully adorned as an exotic bird. Her cloak and tunic were deep purple, spangled with gold; the cloak had an ermine lining and black-and-white sable around the neck. Golden hair framed a face as perfect as if a master craftsman had carved it from ivory. A rosy glow, like crimson reflected by silver, gave warmth to her pale skin. Her nose was slender and perfectly shaped; dark eyebrows arched over sparkling gray eyes. A more beautiful woman never lived, and any man who saw her must surely lose his heart.

She welcomed the knight to her home, and he then exchanged greetings with her companions. The young woman took her guest by the hand and, with great courtesy, said, "My lord, your lodgings tonight will be entirely unworthy of you. If I told you our sad story, you would think I was trying to drive you away. But please, come with me, and accept our hospitality, such as it is; may God grant you better tomorrow!"

And so, still holding him by the hand, she led him to a fine, spacious room with a brightly painted ceiling. A silk counterpane had been draped over the bed on which the two of them sat down. A number of knights accompanied them but stayed quietly at a distance. They watched the stranger sitting beside their lady. He had yet to utter a word, for Gornemant's advice was still fresh in his mind.

"This is very strange," said one. "Why doesn't he say anything?"

"What a pity if his manners don't match his looks!"

"Yes, to look at them, you would think God had made them for each other."

But the young woman, having waited patiently for her guest to break the silence, realized she would have to do it for him.

"Tell me, my lord, where did you come from today?"

"Lady, I spent last night at the home of a wise and kind man where I was very well looked after. The castle had five strong towers, one much taller than the others. I don't know what the place is called, but my host was Gornemant of Gorhaut."

"Ah! How happy I am to hear that! He is the noblest man in the world! I am his niece and know him very well, though I have not seen him for a long time. I am sure he made you very welcome—he is as hospitable as he is wealthy. Here we can offer you only meager fare. Another of my uncles, a priest, kindly sent us some bread for supper tonight, and there is still a small cask of mulled wine. One of my men killed a deer today, so we will have a little meat."

She ordered that tables be brought, and soon everyone sat down to supper. The food was not abundant, but they all enjoyed what there was. After dinner, those who had stood watch the night before were relieved of their duty; others would stay up to guard the castle. Servants saw to the needs of their guest. Fine soft sheets were brought, an elegant coverlet, and a pillow for his head. Every comfort a man can enjoy in bed was his that night, save the company of a maiden or a lady. But he knew nothing of such delights, and was soon fast asleep.

His hostess did not fare so well. She tossed and turned in her bed, thinking of her desolate lands, and that she was now defenseless against attack. At last she could endure it no longer; she felt she must tell her guest what was troubling her. Desperation giving her courage, she jumped up, threw a cloak over her shift, and left the room. She was so terrified at her own daring that her whole body trembled, her skin cold with fear. With her last strength she reached the knight's bed and fell to her knees beside his sleeping form. He awoke to find her arms around his neck, his face wet with her tears. He pulled her close to him whispering, "Beautiful lady, why are you weeping?"

"Ah, noble knight, have mercy! I beg you not to think ill of me because I have come here like this, in such disarray. There is no one in the world as unhappy as I am. This is the last night I have to live. Tomorrow will be my last day. My castle has been besieged for nearly a year by Clamadeus of the Isles. I had a hundred knights, but fifty have been killed or put in prison, and those will die just as surely. I grieve for the many brave men who tried to protect me from an evil fate! Our supplies are now exhausted. Unless God prevents it, we will have to surrender tomorrow, and I will be handed over to Clamadeus. But he will only have my dead body! There is a good steel dagger hidden in my jewel case, and I will thrust it into my heart. That is what I came here to tell you. Farewell!"

Now the knight will have a chance to show his valor, if he dares! The tears that fell on his face were meant to awaken in him a desire to defend her lands, to save her. He said, "Dear one, do not weep any more! Tomorrow need not be the way you imagine. Dry your tears, and come lie here beside me. This bed is certainly wide enough for us both. Stay with me tonight."

"If you wish it, I will."

He took her in his arms and kissed her, gently drawing her under the covers. She was content to have it so, certain that he would do nothing to displease her. All night long they lay in each other's arms.

At dawn the maiden returned to her room and dressed without awakening her servants. As the household began to stir, she went back to the young knight and said, "Good day to you, sir! You must be eager to be on your way! I certainly have no right to complain of that, but I do regret that we couldn't be better hosts. I pray that God will grant you more comfort tonight."

"I won't be going anywhere until your lands are at peace! If you allow me to, I will find your enemy and conquer him if I can. If I succeed, I'll ask for your love as my reward. I want nothing else."

Smiling, she said, "You would certainly have what you ask for, unworthy though it may be. But there is no way for you to defeat my enemy. You would have to fight Clamadeus's seneschal Enguigeron, who is older and more experienced than you are. You must not give up your life for me!"

"I'll challenge him this very day! Nothing will change my mind!"

She tried again and again to make him heed her advice, thus inspiring him to go against it. He asked for his battle gear, and when he was armed and mounted on his horse, she simply said, "Sir, may God be with you today." Everyone accompanied him to the gate, echoing her prayer.

The enemy army was encamped in a broad valley below the city walls. When their scouts saw a knight in red armor approaching, they hastened to report it. The seneschal was sitting in front of his tent, waiting for the castle to be surrendered, or for some champion to defend it in single combat. He was ready for battle, his men already rejoicing at their victory. Astride a powerful warhorse, he rode out to confront the young knight and said, "Who sent you, boy? Have you come to ask for peace or for a fight?"

"What are *you* doing here! Why have you killed so many knights and ruined these lands?"

"My lord is waiting for the surrender of this castle, and he will have the girl as well."

"We'll see about that!"

"So we will."

They lowered their lances and charged. So great was their strength and skill that both lances snapped in two. Enguigeron was hurled to the ground, hitting his shield and bruising his arm and ribs. The young knight, disdaining to remain on horseback, dismounted, sword in hand. The battle was long, and countless blows were exchanged, but at last the seneschal fell.

The boy was upon him in an instant. When his foe cried out for mercy, he shouted, "Never!" But the words of Gornemant came into his mind, and Enguigeron, seeing him hesitate, said, "Be merciful, my friend! You have won. Who would have believed that you could defeat me! Think how your fame will increase when I and all my men bear witness to your valor! If you are in the service of some lord, send me to him. I will tell how you triumphed over me in single combat, and declare myself his prisoner."

"So be it. I would do wrong to ask for more. You must go to my lady, here in this castle, and swear that never in your life will you threaten her again and that your fate is in her hands."

"You might as well kill me right now, since that is what she will do. She hates me more than anyone in the world! Her father died by my hand, and I have killed many of her knights; many others are my prisoners. Unless you want to send me to my death, choose someone else."

"Then go and surrender to Gornemant of Gorhaut."

"I would not be safe there either," said Enguigeron, "since I killed his brother in this war."

"Then you must give yourself up to King Arthur. Greet him for me, and have him point out the maiden Kay slapped. You will declare yourself her prisoner, and say to her that if God keeps me alive, she shall have her revenge."

Enguigeron said he would certainly do all this.

The victorious knight turned toward the castle he had freed. The seneschal gathered his army together and, with his standard bearer in the lead, set off for King Arthur's court. Everyone rushed from Beaurepaire to welcome the knight. They joyfully helped him off with his armor, but they were greatly disappointed that he had not cut off Enguigeron's head while he had the chance. Soon the maiden was at his side and led him off to her chamber where she had not the least objection to his kissing and embracing her. They felt no need to eat or drink—they had all the refreshment they required!

Meanwhile Clamadeus, already on his way to occupy the castle, met a

messenger coming to tell him the grievous news. Clamadeus could not believe that his seneschal had been overcome in battle. "Alas, my lord, it is
true. He has been sent as a prisoner to King Arthur. I do not know the name
of the knight who fought him, but he rode out of Beaurepaire wearing red
armor."

Clamadeus said, "This is not the end! I know they are starving in there.
The knights must be too weak to fight, but we are still strong and well
equipped. All we have to do is send twenty men to challenge them. This
hero, who must be enjoying himself with Blanchefleur, will want to impress
her. He will be quick to attack, but the others won't be able to give him
much help. Our men will draw them on, and then the rest of us, hidden in
that valley, will rush out and overwhelm them."

Soon twenty knights, with all their banners flying, appeared before the
castle. At the young knight's command, the doors were flung open, and he
rode out to confront them. His lance was everywhere, piercing, stabbing,
disemboweling. But then the army, fourteen hundred strong, advanced from
the valley and rushed wildly toward the gate. The defenders held their
ground for a short while but were soon obliged to retreat into the castle.
Archers continued to shoot at the crowd of Clamadeus's men, who were
frantically trying to force their way inside. Just as the first of these broke

through, the great iron gate came crashing down. Clamadeus, dismayed by his losses, had no choice but to withdraw.

One of his counselors said, "My lord, even great men have setbacks. Who can fathom God's will? But if a storm is beating down on you now, soon the sun will shine. I would wager my eyes that the castle will be yours within three days. All you have to do is wait, and she who has been so stubborn will beg you, of your grace, to take her."

They set up their tents and made themselves as comfortable as they could. Those in the castle disarmed their captives. Instead of putting them in irons or locking them up, they simply made them swear they would do no harm and not try to escape. That very day, a great wind arose, driving a barge up the coast. It was filled with wheat and other provisions, and came, as if by a miracle, right up to the castle. Those inside sent hastily to inquire what boat it was and where it came from.

"We are merchants, selling food. We have bread and wine, salt bacon, oxen, and pigs. Do you need anything?"

"God be praised for sending you here! We will buy everything on board— just name your price! If need be, we will pay for the wheat with plates of silver and gold and give you a cartload of treasure for meat and wine."

The merchants set to work unloading the cargo, and those within the castle walls soon had reason to rejoice. The food was prepared in no time. Clamadeus, brooding outside, soon realized that he would have a long wait. And the young knight, for his part, was free to enjoy the lady's company. He held her in his arms, joyfully giving and receiving kisses. Sounds of merriment came from the feasting in the hall. Clamadeus was furious; had his long siege been for nothing? Without consulting his advisors, he sent a messenger to the castle, challenging the Red Knight to single combat. He would wait for him on the empty plain until noon the next day.

When the maiden heard the news, she was distraught and pleaded with him not to go. Her people also did what they could to dissuade him, for no one had ever defeated Clamadeus in battle. "Enough!" said the young knight. "I have made up my mind, and nothing will change it."

They realized it was useless, and everyone sadly retired for the night. When they were alone, the maiden tried to convince him that he need not take up the challenge; after all, Clamadeus had already been defeated. A magical sweetness filled her voice; her every word was accompanied by a kiss, turning the key of love in the lock of his heart. But his resolve remained firm, and in the morning he called for his armor, mounted his horse, and set out, leaving his despairing friends behind.

When Clamadeus saw him coming, he smiled to himself. It would be no trouble at all to knock this boy to the ground. The two of them were alone on the field. They lowered their lances and charged in such murderous rage that their shields crashed together and the lances splintered. The shock felled them both. They were on their feet in an instant, unsheathed their swords, and struck. Clamadeus was astonished to discover that his young opponent was just as accomplished as he was. They did indeed seem perfectly matched in skill, but their combat went on for so long that the younger man's superior endurance began to prevail. At last Clamadeus had to beg for mercy. Like his seneschal, he agreed to surrender only to King Arthur, and to give the young knight's message to the maiden who had laughed. All the prisoners he held would be released, safe and sound, and henceforth he would leave Blanchefleur and her people in peace. Great was the rejoicing in Beaurepaire! Church bells pealed in celebration, people old and young danced in the streets, and every monk and nun gave thanks to God.

It was the custom at that time for vanquished knights to deliver themselves to their captors just as they appeared after battle. Clamadeus therefore left immediately for Disnadaron in Wales, where Arthur was holding court. Three days later, Enguigeron saw him arrive, all covered with blood. The seneschal turned to those around him and said, "My lords, I can hardly believe my eyes! The Red Knight must have defeated my master Clamadeus, the best knight in the world!" He rushed to greet him, and together they entered the hall.

The court was celebrating the Feast of Pentecost. Everyone had just returned from mass and a great crowd of noble visitors was present. The queen sat next to King Arthur on the dais; other kings, queens, dukes, and countesses were entering the hall. Kay arrived, wearing a cloth cap on his braided blond hair. He was cloakless and held a slender staff in his hand. His tunic was of richly dyed red silk, with a beautifully woven belt fastened with gold. There wasn't a handsomer or a braver knight in the world, but he had such an unpleasant disposition that everyone avoided him as he walked through the hall.

It was time to eat but, as was his custom, the king declared that he would not dine until some great news was announced. At just that moment, Clamadeus came in, ready to surrender.

"May God protect the noblest and most generous king alive! The whole world praises your good deeds. Hear me, Sire! I declare myself your prisoner! I was defeated by a knight whose name I do not know. He was wearing red armor that he said was a gift from you."

"Tell me the truth, my friend! Is he well?"

"Yes, I can promise you that. He is the most valiant knight I have ever met, and he asked me to say to the maiden who laughed—the one Kay shamefully struck—that, God willing, he would avenge her."

The jester, hearing these words, jumped for joy and cried out, "Kay will soon pay for that blow! His arm will be broken and his shoulder pulled from its socket." Kay could barely restrain his anger, but the king shook his head and said, "If it weren't for you, that boy would be here with me now!"

The king asked Girflet and Yvain to accompany Clamadeus and Enguigeron to the queen's chambers, where they would find the maiden who laughed. Her injuries had healed, but the shame of them had not, and she was glad to hear the young knight's message.

As Clamadeus swore his allegiance to Arthur, the one who had fought him for the land and for the lady Blanchefleur was lying happily by her side. He could have stayed and ruled her country, had he wished, but the thought of his mother made him uneasy. He could not rest until he saw her again, though the maiden pleaded with him not to leave her. Finally he promised that if he found his mother alive, he would bring her back with him; if not, he would return alone and rule the land.

On his way out of the city, he encountered a large procession of veiled nuns and monks in their ceremonial robes. They were all weeping, and when he approached they said, "Sir, you rescued us from ruin, restored our homes to us! It is a bitter thing to see you leaving."

He replied, "God willing, I'll return very soon. Don't you think it is right for me to go and see my mother? I left her at our home in the Deserted Forest. But I will come back, and bring her with me if she is still alive. If she has died, we will hold a yearly service, asking God to receive her soul among the blessed saints. I promise you, all will be well."

And so they parted. The young knight, fully armed, rode through the forest all day long, praying that God would let him find his mother in good health. There was a river, so fast and deep he dared not try to cross it, but he walked along the bank until his way was blocked by an outcropping of rock. A boat with two men in it came into view. After a moment, he realized the boat was anchored; one of the men was baiting a hook. He called out, "Tell me, my lords, how can I cross this river?"

The one who was fishing answered, "I'm sorry, brother, but for twenty leagues in either direction, there is neither ford nor ferry."

"Can you tell me, then, where I might find lodging?"

"You may stay with me tonight. Take that path up the cliff, and when you are at the top, you will see my house in a valley, close to the river and woods."

The boy rode up the cliff, but all he could see was the forest and empty sky. He was angry, believing he had been sent on a fool's errand, but suddenly there appeared the top of a gray stone tower, not far away in the valley. Then he saw two smaller towers connected by a great stone building. With no more reproaches to the fisherman, the boy rode toward the drawbridge which led to the gate. The bridge was down, and he rode right in. Four squires came running to greet him. Two helped him off with his armor, the third took his horse to a stable, the fourth placed a fine new wool cloak around his shoulders. They took him to a beautifully appointed room where he waited until two servants came and escorted him to the great square hall. Four massive columns in the center of the room supported the bronze mantel of a fireplace; four hundred men could have been comfortably seated around it! A handsome gray-haired nobleman was reclining on a couch, close to the fire. He was dressed in fine dark clothes and wore a sable hat on his head. When he saw the young man, he said, "Please forgive me, sir, for not getting up. It is difficult for me to do so."

"My lord, it is very kind of you to receive me."

The nobleman raised himself as best he could, invited the young man to sit right next to him, and asked where he had been that day. The boy said he had come from Beaurepaire.

"Then you left before daybreak!"

"No indeed, it was much later."

As they were speaking together, a squire entered, bringing the nobleman a beautiful new sword. Its hilt was made of Arabian gold, its baldric of woven silk; Venetian brocade covered its leather sheath. The squire said, "My lord, your niece sends you this gift. She hopes you will offer it to a worthy knight. The man who forged this sword made only three of them, and this one is the last. He said it would never break, unless it was used unworthily."

The nobleman took the sword and handed it to the boy, saying, "Surely this sword was meant for you. Put it on."

The boy did so, thanking him. Then he drew the blade, admired it, and slipped it back into the sheath. The grip fitted his hand perfectly. He entrusted the sword to the servant who had taken charge of his arms. While he and the nobleman were talking, a squire came into the hall carrying a white lance. He passed in front of the fire, and the light shone on a bright red drop of blood running down from the tip all the way to his hand. The boy was filled with wonder at this extraordinary sight, but he remembered how Gornemant had warned him about talking too much, and he dared not ask any questions. Then two more squires came in, holding candelabras enameled in brilliant colors; at least ten candles burned in each. After the squires came a maiden who held in her outstretched hands a golden grail adorned with the richest jewels in all the world. So great was its radiance that the light of the candles was eclipsed like that of stars when the moon rises. A second maiden followed, carrying an oval carving dish made of a silver so pure it seemed to glow from within. The procession passed through the room, and the boy remained silent.

The host asked the servants to bring warm water and towels. When he and the boy had washed their hands, two squires appeared with a broad ivory board which they placed on ebony trestles and covered with a magnificent white tablecloth. The first course was venison with a spicy pepper sauce. A squire carved the meat on the silver dish and served it on thick slices of bread. Delicious wines were poured into golden goblets. The maiden holding the grail passed through the room several times, but still the boy was silent. He longed to know who was being served from the grail but feared it would be impolite to ask. He decided to wait until morning when he said good-bye to his host.

The feast went on and on, but at last the squires left to prepare the beds and the midnight fruit. There were dates and figs spiced with nutmeg and cloves, pomegranates, Alexandrian ginger, and various drinks soothing to the stomach. "It is time I went to bed, my dear friend," said the host, "but you, of course, may stay up as long as you like." Four strong servants grasped the corners of the coverlet on which the nobleman reclined, and bore him away.

Squires saw to the boy's needs, helping him off with his clothes and preparing a bed with fine linen sheets. When he awoke at dawn he found himself all alone. He dressed and was surprised to find his armor there in the hall. He put it on as best he could. The doors of the adjoining chambers, which had been open the night before, were now shut tight. He tried them all, knocking and shouting, but no one came and no one replied. Nothing broke the deep silence of the hall. Only the great door leading to the outside remained open. At the bottom of the stairs he found his horse, already saddled, and his lance and shield leaning against a mounting block nearby. He mounted and searched everywhere but didn't see a soul. The drawbridge was down, and he began to ride across it, thinking he might find the squires out hunting in the forest. He hoped one of them would explain about the bleeding lance and the grail. But before he reached the end of the bridge, he felt the back of his horse rise up underneath him. It made a great leap, nearly unseating him, and just managed to land on the other side, saving them both from harm. When the boy turned around to see what had happened, the drawbridge was already raised. He called out repeatedly, shouting with all his might, but no one answered.

When, at last, he rode off into the forest, he saw hoofprints and followed them eagerly. Surely the squires from the castle had gone that way! But the tracks led to an oak tree, beneath which sat a maiden who cradled in her lap the head of a dead knight. She was weeping and lamenting, "If only I could have died in his place! What good is life to me, without my love?"

The boy approached and asked the maiden what had happened. "A knight cut his throat," she said, "this very morning."

Despite her grief, she noticed that the boy and his horse looked as if they'd had good lodging, even though there was nowhere to stay for forty leagues in any direction—unless he had been the guest of the Fisher King! When she asked him about that, he said, "I don't know, but I did see a man fishing from a boat, and he said I could stay at his house."

"He is indeed a king, but he was terribly wounded and cannot ride anymore. When he wants to divert himself he goes fishing, and that is why he is called the Fisher King."

"Just the same, he asked me to sit right next to him and even apologized for not getting up to greet me!"

"He did you great honor indeed. But tell me, did you see the lance with the bleeding tip?"

"Yes!"

"And did you ask how a wooden lance could bleed?"

"No. I thought it would be rude."

"That was very wrong of you. And you must have seen the maiden bearing the grail. Did you ask what that meant?"

"No, I did not."

"That is a great pity. Tell me, what is your name?"

And he who had never known whether he had a name or not, answered without hesitation, "I am Perceval of Wales."

"Then your name has changed, my friend! You are Perceval the Worthless! If only you had asked about the grail, the king's wounds would have been healed and countless blessings would have followed! Now misfortune will come to you and to many others. This is a punishment for your selfishness. Your mother died of sorrow when you left her all alone. You don't remember me, but I am your cousin, and I lived in your mother's house when I was a child. Our kinship makes me grieve all the more for your failure, as sad for me as the death of this knight I loved."

"Cousin, how do you know my mother is dead?"

"I saw her body put into the ground."

"May God have mercy on her soul! I was going home to see her, and now it is too late. But maybe I could be of use to *you*. It's no good staying here watching over a dead knight—he can give you no protection. We should leave the dead to the dead and seek out his killer. I promise I will fight him until one of us surrenders."

"I will remain with my friend until he has been buried. If you truly want to avenge me, there is the path the knight took when he left. But I did not mean for you to risk your life."

She remained to grieve for her dead knight, and Perceval went his way. He rode along for a time, following the hoofprints of another horse that he soon overtook. It was a pathetic beast, painfully thin, with drooping ears and a scraggly mane; it trembled as if with cold. On the horse's emaciated back sat a maiden, and never was one more wretched. Despite her suffering, you could still see that she was beautiful. Her dress was so tattered that her bare breasts showed through, even though the fabric had been knotted or stitched together in many places. Her skin was deeply scratched and had been burned by sun and wind. Tears ran down her devastated face, spilling onto her ragged clothes. It was heartbreaking to see her.

"Please, dear God," she was saying, "send someone to deliver me from my tormentor! Why does he abuse me like this? You know that I am innocent! And even if I weren't, if he cared about me at all, he would long since have forgiven me."

When Perceval approached, she began to pull at her garments, trying to cover her nakedness, but as soon as one hole was closed, a dozen others opened up.

"Lovely lady, God be with you!"

She lowered her eyes and said softly, "God's blessing on you, my lord, though I certainly have no reason to wish you well."

"Why do you say that?" said Perceval, taken aback. "I have never done you any harm!"

"All that I am suffering is your fault!"

"Please tell me what you mean!"

"Have mercy, my lord! Go away and leave me in peace! Go while you can!"

"But why?"

"The Proud Knight kills any man who speaks to me. He killed one just this morning."

At that very moment, a knight burst out of the woods and came thundering up to them, shouting at the top of his voice, "How dare you talk to her! You shall die for this! But first you'll hear how wicked she is! One day, I went riding in the forest, leaving this maiden behind in my tent. While I was gone, some Welsh fellow happened upon her. Bad enough that he helped himself to my wine and food, and took my ring off her finger! But he also forced her to kiss him, and we all know what came next! A woman who allows herself to be kissed won't stop at that! Even if she fights and scratches, it's only for show. She's just afraid to admit what she really wants. That's how I know he had his way with her. Until I cut off his head, my lady shall suffer for her betrayal."

Perceval listened in silence. Then he said, "Her punishment is over. I am the one who took her ring and kissed her against her will."

"Then you deserve to die!"

"My death may not be quite as near as you think."

Without another word they wheeled their horses and charged with such rage that both lances splintered. The two knights fell crashing to the ground but were on their feet in an instant, swords in hand. The Proud Knight struck at once, knocking precious stones and enamel flowers from Perceval's helmet. Then the battle began in earnest, both knights fighting with all their might. Many blows were exchanged until at last the Proud Knight declared himself vanquished. He pleaded for his life, and Perceval, always mindful of Gornemant's counsel, said, "I will have mercy on you when you have mercy on this lady! She never deserved what you have made her suffer."

And the knight, who really loved her, replied, "My lord, I will gladly do whatever you ask. I hate myself for having been so unjust."

"Then accompany her to your closest house and make sure she rests and has warm baths so that her health may be fully restored. After that you must conduct her, suitably dressed, to King Arthur. You will declare yourself his prisoner, defeated by the one who became the Red Knight. Then you will tell the assembled court how you punished this innocent maiden, and say to the seneschal Kay that I will never again come to King Arthur's court until I have avenged the girl who laughed."

When the Proud Knight surrendered to King Arthur and told his story, Sir Gawain, who had recently returned to court, wondered aloud who this extraordinary knight could be. His uncle, the king, told him about the unknown boy who had seemed of gentle birth, and how Kay had maliciously said he could have the Red Knight's armor. Now the king swore he would not spend two nights in one place until he learned what had become of him.

Soon the long baggage train was assembled, its carts and packhorses laden with all the equipment the court would need. Arthur set out from Carlion in great pomp, accompanied by his knights, the queen, and her ladies. That night they set up their tents in a frozen meadow; when they awoke, everything was covered with snow. As it happened, Perceval was riding in just that direction. When he neared the king's encampment, he heard the cry of wild geese and, looking up, he saw them, with a falcon in swift pursuit. One of the geese lagged behind the others; the falcon struck, and its prey fell to the ground. Perceval went to look and found nothing but three drops of blood seeping into the snow. He gazed, entranced, at the delicate mingling of red and white; it reminded him of the blush on Blanchefleur's cheeks. He sat there on his horse, lost in revery. One of Arthur's squires thought he must be asleep and pointed him out to Sagremor, who had just left his tent. Sagremor woke the king, saying, "My lord, there is an armed knight on the other side of the meadow."

"Bring him to me at once."

Sagremor called for his horse and his arms, and galloped off to confront Perceval: "Sir, the king requires your presence."

Perceval, pretending not to have heard, made no answer. Sagremor, who was called Sagremor the Unruly because of his intemperate nature, repeated his message. When there was no reply, he began shouting that he was sorry to have wasted words on such a dolt, and that the knight would come with him whether he wanted to or not. He unfurled the pennant wrapped around his lance and backed up his horse. With a sharp cry of warning, he charged.

Perceval left off his musing and galloped toward his challenger, whose lance broke as they met. He was knocked to the ground, and Arthur's knights saw his horse running toward them. They were all alarmed except Kay, mocking as usual, who said to the king, "See how Sagremor is escorting the knight into your presence!"

"Perhaps you can do better!"

"With great pleasure! I will have him here in no time and find out his name as well."

The seneschal armed in haste and rode toward Perceval, who was again contemplating the drops of blood in the snow. Still at a distance, he shouted, "Vassal, come with me to the king! You will pay for it if you don't!" Not waiting for an answer, he charged the knight, who spurred toward him at great speed. Kay struck with such force that his lance shattered, but Perceval's blow hit the seneschal's helmet and hurled him from his horse. He landed on a rock, dislocating his shoulder, while his upper arm snapped like a piece of dry wood. It was exactly as the jester had predicted. Kay fainted from pain, and his horse trotted off toward the tents. Everyone hurried to look for the seneschal, and when they saw him lying so still, they were sure he had been killed. King Arthur was almost beside himself with grief, for he loved Sir Kay in spite of his bad temper. But a doctor examined the knight and said he would recover, once his shoulder was put back in place and his broken arm splinted. This he accomplished with the help of two maidens he had trained. They put Sir Kay on a litter and carried him to the king's tent, where he soon regained consciousness.

Meanwhile, Perceval had returned to his contemplation. Gawain said to the king, "My lord, you have often told us that a knight who is deep in thought should not be disturbed. Perhaps he is grieving for the loss of a friend or for his beloved. If it please you, I will go and wait until he is less preoccupied. Then, perhaps, I can persuade him to come here with me."

"That is just like you!" said Kay. "How many have you defeated when they were tired from fighting others! You won't even need to draw your sword—you can just stroke him like a cat and he'll follow you."

"Do you think you will get revenge on him by insulting me? I'll bring him here if I can, my friend, and without getting a broken arm for my trouble!"

"Go, by all means, nephew," said the king, "but be careful!"

So Gawain rode out toward the knight, whose gaze was still fixed on the snowy ground. But the drops of blood had almost disappeared, and with them the thoughts of Blanchefleur. Gawain came up to him quietly and said, "Sir, I hope you won't take offence if I greet you. I bring you a message from King Arthur, who would like you to come and speak with him."

"Two of your friends were here already, intending to drag me off to the king as if I were their prisoner. I just wanted to be left alone with my thoughts. There were three drops of blood here in the snow, and they reminded me of the blush on my beloved's face."

"Such thoughts are very worthy, sir. But may I ask what you intend to do now? The king desires your company, and I would gladly take you to him."

"First tell me, is Kay the seneschal there?"

"He certainly is. He's the knight you just defeated, and it cost him dear. He broke his right arm and dislocated his shoulder."

"Then I have avenged the maiden he struck."

Gawain was astonished, and replied, "Sir, you are the very person the king has been looking for! What is your name?"

"Perceval. And what is yours?"

"I am Gawain."

"I have often heard of you, sir, and desired to know you. Of course I'll be very glad to accompany you. Please lead the way."

Soon those who kept watch in the king's encampment saw the two knights crossing the field and heading toward the tents. They had removed their helmets and seemed to be engaged in cheerful conversation. The squires were amazed and ran to tell the king.

"Sire! Sire! Sir Gawain is bringing the knight, and they are *laughing*!"

Only Kay had something unpleasant to say: "Now your nephew Gawain will get all the credit! It must have been quite a battle if he's returning in such a good mood!"

Not wanting to present his new friend to the king while he was still in battle gear, Gawain took Perceval to his tent and offered some of his own elegant clothes. Then they went to greet the king.

"My lord, I bring you the man you have been seeking!"

The king, who had jumped up to greet them, said, "Sir, you are most welcome! Please tell me what we should call you."

"Sire, my name is Perceval of Wales."

"Well, Perceval, now that you have come back to my court, I hope you will never leave it! I have been very worried about you."

As the king was conversing with Perceval, the queen came in. She had heard about the young knight's arrival and brought with her the maiden who had laughed. Perceval greeted the queen, saying, "May God reward you always with joy and honor!"

Guenevere replied, "You have proven your valor far and wide, and you are most welcome here."

Perceval turned to the maiden who had laughed and said, "My lady, if ever you need a champion, I will not fail you."

She thanked him with all her heart. Then the king and queen and the knights joyfully accompanied Perceval back to Carlion, where they celebrated for two whole days and nights. On the third day, a damsel came riding toward them on a tawny mule, brandishing a scourge in her right hand. Believe me, you have never seen such a hideous creature! Her black hair was tied in scraggly braids, and her skin was as dark as an old iron pot. She had little holes for eyes, no bigger than a rat's; her nose was as flat as a monkey's or a cat's, and a little goat beard had sprouted from her chin. With her breastbone jutting out, and a hump on her shoulders, she was hardly a vision of grace!

She rode straight into the hall and warmly greeted the king and all the

knights, except for Perceval. To him she said, "Woe to you, Perceval! Fortune has a forelock, but behind, her head is bald. A curse on anyone who
lets her slip by! You were the guest of the Fisher King; you saw the lance and
the grail. But you would not take the trouble to open your mouth and ask
why a drop of blood ran from the lance's tip! Nor did you bother to inquire
why the grail was carried through the hall. You had all the time in the world,
yet you kept silent. A few words from you would have put an end to the
king's suffering! His wounds would have been healed and he would once
again have ruled his lands! Now that will never happen. His kingdom will
always be a wasteland, wives will lose their husbands and maidens their
hopes, many brave knights will die, and all because of you."

Then the damsel turned to the king and said, "I am on my way to a
castle where more than five hundred knights have gathered. All are eager
to prove their valor, in the presence of their noble ladies. It is a great
opportunity for brave men! But even greater honor will go to the knight
who rescues the Lady of the Golden Circle, who is under siege at Montesclaire!"

With that, she took her leave. Gawain leaped to his feet and said that,
God willing, he would save the maiden. Girflet would try his luck at the
Lofty Castle, and Kaherdin declared that he too would set out in search of
adventure. But Perceval spoke very differently. He would never sleep two
nights in the same place until he found his way back to the Castle of the
Grail and learned the meaning of its mysteries.

And so they parted, each to follow his chosen path.

*   *   *

FIVE SPRINGTIMES WENT BY, five whole years in which Perceval wandered the world, endlessly searching for the river and the hilltop that had shown him the way to the Grail Castle. Sometimes he was sure he saw its gray towers in the distance, but always, as he approached, they disappeared into the mist. Otherwise, the world seemed to offer him nothing but opportunities to demonstrate his valor and knightly skills, and gradually these became his life. He defeated countless worthy opponents and sent them to Arthur's court, but many of his adventures were never known, because there was no one to send.

One day, on top of a high hill, he sat silently on his horse and gazed in wonder at the countryside below. As far as the eye could see, every dwelling had been destroyed, and all the land was charred and black. He rode down into what had once been a dense green forest; now there were only skeletons of trees. He rode all day through the desolation, until at last he came to an open plain. A marble cross had been placed under an isolated tree, close to the statue of a lovely young woman. It was late, and Perceval was exhausted; he decided to go no farther that night. He jumped down and removed the horse's bridle. Fortunately, he did not take off his armor but lay down as he was, next to the cross. Soon the moon rose, clear and bright. After a time, the stillness of the night was interrupted by a lament: "When will I find the one who killed my lady? I have destroyed so many knights! Will I never get a chance to fight the one who is guilty? I can't give up until she is avenged."

The voice fell silent. Perceval rose and swiftly put the bridle on his horse. The next thing he knew, a knight was galloping straight toward him, his eyes blazing with fury. "I'll kill you!" he shouted, "I swear it!"

Perceval replied, "Then you would commit a sin, my lord, for I have never done you any harm."

"Right or wrong, my sword will have your head!"

"We'll see about that!"

"You dare defy me? If there were ten of you, you wouldn't have a chance! Get on your horse!"

Perceval made haste to mount and lace on his helmet. At the first charge, both men were knocked to the ground, but they drew their swords and continued fighting on foot. The night wore on, but still they fought, their steel blades red to the hilt. At last, when they were so exhausted they could hardly breathe, Perceval pinned his opponent to the ground. "It's over! Ask for mercy!"

"I'd rather die!"

Perceval reached down, cut the golden laces of the knight's helmet, and pulled it off. Seeing how young his opponent was, and how desperately sad, he felt pity.

"Tell me who you are, and what has caused you such grief."

"My name is Lugarel, my lord. I was blessed with a wise and worthy sweetheart; this statue is in her likeness. I loved her so much that I took her with me wherever I went. One day, during the feast of St. John, we happened upon this place. I had my tent set up and the floor strewn with freshly cut flowers; then I sent my servants away so that I could be alone with my lady. We were there for eight days, and during that time I jousted with every knight who passed by. I defeated them all! On the ninth day I went out riding and saw a magnificent stag fleeing a hound. I joined in the pursuit and at last ran it down, but while I was away in the forest, a knight arrived at our tent and threatened to kill my lady if she did not do what he asked. When she refused, he stabbed her with his sword and left her there to die. By the time I returned she could hardly speak; she died only moments later. But what could I do? I had no idea who the man was, or where he had gone. My servants heard my cries and came running. Nothing could console me, but after a time I sent them to find a skilled workman to make this statue of my lady, and the cross that marks her grave. When all this had been done, I swore to stay here and kill every man who approached until the murderer returned to the scene of his crime. But now that I've been defeated, and would have been killed had you not spared me, I will become a hermit, and expiate my sins in service to God."

Overcome by profound grief, the knight began to weep. His heart gave way, and he fell dead at Perceval's feet. Feeling too exhausted to begin digging a grave, Perceval decided to keep watch over the body, but before he knew it, he was fast asleep. When he awoke the next morning, the dead knight was nowhere to be seen. Instead he found a beautiful marble tomb on which these words had been inscribed: "Pray for the soul of Lugarel! All true lovers should pity him."

Perceval, totally astonished, crossed himself and prayed that God would protect him from harm. With one last look at the statue, he mounted and rode off into the forest. Absorbed in thoughts of Lugarel, whom he might have killed, he was startled by a woman's voice, speaking words full of woe. "Alas, how sad is my heart! How could I have believed him? Now I know that a handsome face can be a mask for treachery, and golden words hide dark thoughts. What a fool I was to trust him! But now it is too late." When she saw Perceval coming, she reined in her mule.

The knight said, "Lady, may God heal your pain and send you joy."

"May God hear you," she replied, "and may He reward your efforts with better fortune than I have known. If I could find the one I have been searching for so long, I would still have hope. But that will never happen."

Seeing her anguish, Perceval courteously asked her to tell him who it was she sought, and why. She told how a knight named Faradien had proclaimed his love for her, and how she had believed him. "I could not resist the sweetness of his words when he sighed and said he was dying of love for me. He pressed me to do his will, promising to marry me the very next day. What he took from me that night is lost forever. Now he despises me, but I still love him. I have pleaded with him to honor his word, but he will have nothing to do with me. I have only my cousin to help me, but I can't find him anywhere. His name is Perceval, and they say he has gone to look for the grail. But it doesn't matter now. Tomorrow the one I love will marry someone else. I know I will die of sorrow, but it's better than living in grief."

"Tell me about this knight."

"He is so tall and strong that he fears no one. He has never been defeated, and he never tires of fighting."

"I will go with you and see what can be done. He would be a fool to leave you for another."

By the time they reached the church, the priest was saying, "If anyone knows any reason why these two cannot be joined in holy matrimony, let him speak now or forever hold his peace."

Perceval's cousin, emboldened by her love, stepped forward and said, "I have come here to say this man is betrothed to me."

The knight was furious. "If you don't get out right now, I will have you beaten!"

Perceval intervened. "If you please, my lord, show more courtesy to this lady, who has every right to be here and who truly loves you. If you were betrothed to her first, you must honor your promise."

"I will do whatever I like! You'll pay for it if you insist on interfering."

"Threats will get you nowhere," said Perceval. "I intend to prove she is right."

"You must be eager to die, if you want to fight with me!"

The count, who was the knight's overlord, was present, and Perceval asked him to consider the case. He told everything he knew of the matter and declared himself ready to champion the lady's cause. The knight denied it all, and swore he would prove his innocence on the field. He sent for his weapons at once, the battle lines were drawn, and the fight began.

The knight on his great charger was full of confidence. He had never lost a battle in all his life, and Perceval in his old armor did not impress him. Soon their swords were moving faster than the wind, and fragments of helmets and shields flew through the air. Hours passed, and the battle wore on. In the end, Perceval prevailed and his vanquished opponent lay helpless on the ground.

"My lord," he said, "I will do anything you ask. Until today I thought I was the best knight in the world, but I've been proved wrong. It is true what they say: pride goes before a fall."

The count came up to Perceval and asked him who he was. "I am Perceval of Wales," he quietly replied, "and this maiden is my cousin Ysmaine."

"This is an honor indeed, my friend!"

The would-be bride, with bitterness in her heart, mounted and rode away. The count asked Perceval to dine with him, but he declined, preferring to stay and see his cousin wed. Faradien and Ysmaine were led into the chapel and the ceremony was performed, whether the bridegroom was glad about it or not. Perceval told him to go with his wife to King Arthur and say that he had been vanquished by the knight who seeks the grail. Faradien was overjoyed: "It is a greater honor, my lord, to have been defeated by you, than to have struck down every one of the knights of the Round Table!" He and his new wife took their leave and rode away.

The priest invited Perceval to stay and dine with him, and the knight accepted gladly. He washed the blood from his face with warm water and wine and dried it with a white cloth. The priest gave him a warm tunic to put on. They had a simple but abundant dinner, and the count sent over four servants with good red wine.

Then Perceval continued traveling through the forest until the mountainside was so steep and the trees so close together he hardly knew where to turn. He heard a sound and reined in his horse. Right in front of him was a most beautiful maiden, crying as if her heart would break. Perceval rode up close to her and asked if he could help. "Ah, noble knight," she replied, "Please take me away from here! I am Felise, the daughter of Arguisel the Scot. I was walking in a meadow close to my father's castle when two knights seized me, threw me on a horse, and galloped away to this forest. They knocked me to the ground and said I must do their will. I would rather be torn limb from limb! By the grace of God, two other knights rode up and challenged them, and they all started fighting. I didn't wait to see who won! As soon as they weren't looking I got up and ran! I have not eaten or slept in three days. Please take me home! My friends will be very grateful."

Perceval dismounted. If only he could have seen her treachery! This young woman kept watch in the forest until a knight or a peasant came by, and led him into an ambush. She held Perceval in conversation until five robbers sprang out of the woods shouting, "You are our prisoner!"

Perceval leaped on his horse as they surrounded him, demanding that he surrender. He challenged them to fight him one at a time, but they came at him all together. Meeting their charge, he transfixed the first with his lance, right through the chain mail into his heart, and broke the lances of the others against his shield. They all drew their swords, but Perceval slashed through the helmet of one, killing him. The severed arm of another fell to the ground. When the two still alive tried to flee, the girl mocked them for losing, five against one! They fought on for a while, but Perceval felled the last as he tried again to escape. The knight turned back to confront the treacherous girl, but she had vanished. He rode through the woods all day long, seeking her everywhere, to no avail.

At a nearby castle, a whole crowd of people came to greet him. The master of the house was overjoyed to learn the name of his guest. His lady took out a new silk cloak lined with sable and fastened it around Perceval's neck with golden clasps. They offered him a fine meal, honoring him as the most valiant knight in the world. When they heard about his encounter with the robbers, they were even more delighted. They and other landowners in the district had very often suffered from their depredations. That night, after a last drink of wine, which his host served to Perceval in a goblet of pure gold, the knight slept soundly in a fine bed. Although the people of the castle hoped that he would stay longer, "at least a week or two," said their lord, Perceval had his horse made ready early the next morning and rode away.

That night he shared the meager food of two hermits, and his bed was only fresh straw on the hard ground. In the morning he went to mass in their little chapel, and then he confessed his sins as best he could. The priest's response was unexpected: "I cannot consider it wise to wear out the body only to lose the soul. Warfare and murder are not the business of knights, who should serve the cause of justice and defend the Holy Church. Give up your childish ways, if you seek the love of God."

Perceval promised to try, and the priest blessed him when he took his leave. Once again on the forest paths, he let his horse choose the way. It took the path to the right, and Perceval prayed that God would keep him on the right road and lead him to the home of the Fisher King. Thinking of the years he had spent in his quest, all the blows he had endured, the hardships and suffering, he wondered how much longer he could continue. And perhaps he was too unworthy ever to be again in the presence of the grail. Perhaps he was wasting his life in a hopeless dream. And yet there was nothing else for him to do.

One day, as he was riding along, armed as usual from head to toe, he happened upon three knights and ten ladies. Their hoods were drawn down over their heads, and they were walking barefoot, garbed in penitential shirts of stiff horsehair. They were all astonished by Perceval's appearance, and one of the knights requested him to stop.

"My friend, do you not believe in Jesus Christ? It is a sin to carry arms on the day he died."

Perceval, confused, replied, "Excuse me, sir, what day is this?"

"What day! Don't you know? This is Good Friday, when we should worship the Cross and pray for forgiveness of our sins! Our Lord died today, betrayed for thirty pieces of silver. His death is our salvation; through him we have eternal life. Christians should put down their weapons and do penance on this day."

"Where have you come from?"

"A saintly hermit lives here in the forest. To him we have made our confessions and asked for God's forgiveness."

Tears came to Perceval's eyes. "I would go see this holy man," he said, "if I knew the way."

"Sir, you have only to follow this path. Go through these woods, and you will see the markers we have tied to the branches. We put them there so that no one would get lost."

They commended one another to God, and Perceval, still weeping, turned his horse onto the path they had shown him. When he arrived at the hermit's dwelling, he dismounted and put down his weapons, then tied his horse to an elm tree. A small chapel had been constructed in a clearing, and there Perceval found the hermit. A priest and his young acolyte were with him, preparing to begin the service. The knight fell to his knees, and the holy man, seeing his distress, asked how he could help him.

"Five years ago I was the guest of the Fisher King, and while I was there I saw a lance that bled. Truly, a drop of blood ran down from the tip! And then I saw a grail, and a marvelous light shone from it. I wanted to ask about these things, but I didn't dare. When I learned that my silence had been wrong, I was so unhappy I wanted to die. I've been trying all this time to find my way back to that place, but now I think I will never see it again."

"What is your name, my friend?"

"Perceval."

The hermit sighed, for he knew the name well. "The one who is served from the grail is my brother, and the Fisher King is his son. Your mother was our sister. When you rode away from home, you saw her fall. If you had returned to comfort her, she might still be alive. You thought only of yourself. You were wrong not to care about your mother, and wrong not to ask about the grail."

"Uncle, please tell me how I can make amends."

"You must believe in God, and worship him. Go to church every morning, if you possibly can. Honor all worthy men and women. Always help people in need, especially widows and orphans. Now if you will stay here with me for two days, I will teach you what I can."

The hermit whispered the words of a prayer, repeating it several times so that Perceval would know it by heart. In this prayer were many names for our Lord, powerful names that must never be said aloud except in time of greatest need. Then Perceval, filled with joy, worshiped in the chapel. When evening came, he ate what his uncle did, lettuce, watercress, and barley bread. They drank water from a clear stream. And on Easter Sunday, the young knight took communion.

Perceval left the next morning, newly resolved to find the Fisher King. Commending himself to God, he followed trackless ways into the forest.

When at last he emerged into the open, he found himself in a lovely meadow. Presently he saw, curving away in front of him, a crenelated wall, half red and half white. He wondered who lived inside its enclosure, and rode around until he found a door. It was closed tight. He knocked and shouted for someone to come, but there was no reply except for sounds of festivity within. From flutes, harps and vielles—or perhaps it was human voices— came a music so compelling and so sweet that Perceval forgot every sorrow he had ever known. He knocked again, shouting, "Hurry up and let me in!" No one answered. Enraged, the knight unsheathed the Fisher King's sword and began to pound its hilt against the door.

The response was swift. A bolt of lightning split the sky and thunder crashed in his ears. The sword, ripped from his hand, fell to the ground, the blade broken in two. Perceval was still staring at it in astonishment when the door was opened a crack, and an old man looked out, saying, "How dare you disturb us!"

"Fair lord, I beg you to open the door all the way! The music is so wonderful, and there is such a glorious light inside!"

"That is all you can know of it for now. Perhaps someday that light will be shown to you fully."

"Ah! my lord, tell me what I must do."

"All that you desire could come to you easily, but the sinful man toils in vain, believing that worthy deeds, reputation, and his own strength and valor will bring him to the joy that is eternal. I can also tell you this: your sword will repair itself at the time when you need it most, and when you know how to use it." With that he closed the door.

Perceval picked up the pieces of his sword and put them in its scabbard. He turned the head of his horse and rode slowly across the meadow. After a moment, he stopped and looked behind him. The open ground stretched out endlessly; the enclosing walls were nowhere to be seen.

*   *   *

TOWARD NOONTIME Perceval emerged from the forest and found himself in a fertile plain, golden with ripening wheat. He rode on into orchards whose trees were laden with fruit. He had not seen a land so rich for a very long time. In the distance, the towers of a castle, elegant and fine, were etched on the horizon. After a while, he came to a drawbridge that took him across the river flowing along the base of the ramparts. Inside the castle walls was a large town with two abbeys and several large churches whose iron bells rang the hours. The streets were full of richly dressed men and women. Merchants plied their wares, and you could buy from them whatever your heart desired: furs, horses, gold and silver dishes, jewelry, wax, metal pots, foreign coins, and all manner of oriental spices. Great quantities of precious silks had been imported from Alexandria and Babylon, Cairo, Antioch and Acre. At the steps of the castle, four young squires made Perceval welcome and led him into the great hall, where a beautiful young woman came running to greet him, crying, "My lord, you have come home at last!" And then they were clasped in each other's arms.

When Blanchefleur could speak again, she addressed the astonished knights and ladies around her: "Here is Perceval, the valiant knight who saved me and my lands from Clamadeus! Welcome him as your rightful lord and do him every honor!"

Soon the happy news had spread throughout the castle and the town. Church bells rang, incense filled the air, silk draperies embroidered with gold hung from every window. The entire day was passed in celebration, and when nightfall came, everyone in Beaurepaire feasted in the great hall, brilliant with candlelight. Now Perceval was where he belonged, with the one he loved most in the world. A benevolent fate had led him back to the place he had longed for in his endless wanderings. Musicians played all evening, delighting everyone, and the laughter and talking went on until midnight when the guests went home and servants readied the room for the night. Blanchefleur led Perceval to an elegant bedchamber, paneled in fine wood, and then went to her own room which was close by. But when the candles were extinguished and the exhausted household slept, she slipped from her bed and went to her beloved. He was wide awake, waiting for her, and when they lay side by side she said, "Do not think ill of me for coming to you like this. I have waited so long, desiring you more with every passing day." Perceval took her in his arms and covered her face with kisses.

They slept very little that night, and they talked of many things. Perceval said that he had not even recognized Beaurepaire, so completely was it transformed. She explained that after he had gone, "I knew not where, to seek still more fame," she had felt terribly alone, without anyone to depend on should misfortune come again. She could not prevent her thoughts from dwelling on her fears and became so sad she truly wished to die. But gradually her knights returned from Clamadeus's prison, and all the people the war had driven from her lands came home again. She asked those who knew about such matters to recommend masons and carpenters, and so the broken walls were rebuilt, and fine new towers replaced the ones destroyed. "Now a thousand knights will do you homage as their lord when we are married."

"Beloved," said Perceval, "I cannot stay with you now, but I promise to come back as soon as I can. First I must honor my quest."

"And yet, my lord, honor is also due the promise you made when you left, saying that you would go to see your mother and then return to be the lord of these lands. Because of that, I have waited all this time, and indeed I will wait again, for I love you so much I would suffer anything rather than try to keep you from your desire."

She held him tight and kissed him many times, then said, with grief in her heart, "Come and go when you wish, but stay with me now for just two days."

Reluctantly, Perceval agreed. It was nearly morning, and Blanchefleur embraced him once more, giving no sign of her distress. Then she went back to her bed where, exhausted, she fell asleep. But she was up and beautifully dressed before the bells rang for mass. She had one of her maidens bring Perceval a gold-embroidered tunic which he wore when he entered the great hall. Many knights had assembled there, and they greeted him joyfully, doing him honor as their lord. He returned their welcome, then went to meet Blanchefleur as she came in, dressed in deep blue samite embroidered with gold flowers and silver stars. Her ermine-lined cloak was of the same rare silk. Together they went to hear mass in the chapel, but they themselves were so beautiful that many who should have been listening to the priest were diverted by the pleasure of their eyes.

After mass they returned to the hall with the many knights and ladies who joined them for an elegant meal, with spiced nuts and fruit for dessert. As long as Perceval stayed in Beaurepaire, he saw only smiling faces; sadness seemed to be banished from the world. But after two days he had his armor brought to him, and his warhorse, richly equipped with a new saddle and bridle. Blanchefleur wept and gently urged him to stay a little longer. He begged her not to be sad and not to be afraid. "I'll return to you, my love, as soon as I can."

Blanchefleur could not speak, her heart was so oppressed, but noblemen of her household gave voice to her private thoughts when they asked the knight not to leave before he married their lady, wise and rich and beautiful

as she was. He vowed that once he had accomplished his quest, he would return and stay in Beaurepaire for the rest of his life. With that he mounted and rode away.

*   *   *

PERCEVAL TRAVELED through lands that seemed entirely deserted, until one day he encountered two weeping maidens and a knight who was being carried on a litter. The knight's legs and thighs had been badly burned.

Perceval tried to find out what had happened to him, but the maidens could tell him nothing through their tears. So Perceval journeyed on, absorbed in his thoughts. Before long he encountered a squire accompanying a knight whose head and neck were similarly burned. Perceval asked questions of the squire, but he too turned away, weeping bitterly. Wondering what lay ahead to explain such terrible wounds, he continued along a narrow, half over-grown path, until it was nearly dark. Then a light in the distance meant, he hoped, that he and his horse could find lodging for the night.

He saw an open door leading into a courtyard. From there he entered the house, where he found thirteen monks, as pale as if they never went out-doors. A servant had just cut a loaf of bread into thirteen pieces, while another man stood beside the abbot. The lighted candle he held provided the only illumination. They were about to eat their meager supper when they were suprised by the arrival of an armed horseman in their midst. Perceval greeted them courteously and asked if they would be willing to give him lodging for the night: "I have searched long and hard and found no other place."

"You will not find much comfort here," said a servant.

"Shelter is all I need."

The abbot, who looked like a great nobleman in spite of his worn mo-nastic robe, invited Perceval to dismount, and a servant led his horse away to a stable. They helped the knight with his armor, led him to a place beside the fire, and offered him a generous share of their food, although it was barely enough to keep body and soul together. He spoke to those around him, but no one replied. A servant explained that only the abbot ever talked, and then it was to greet their rare guests. But he would speak to Perceval in the morning, and the knight could ask his advice, if he so desired. Then the servant showed him to a cell-like room where he spent the night on a thin straw pallet.

At dawn he heard mass in a little chapel, and then the abbot took him aside and asked if he could help him in any way. Feeling that one who lived so holy a life might be able to explain something that troubled him, Perceval related his encounter with the old man near the wall where he broke his sword. That man had told him that knightly deeds were not pleasing to God. And after he killed the robbers, a priest had said the same thing. "Should I have left those wicked men in peace, and that lying girl, to work their evil?"

"A knight's deeds are his glory," said the abbot, "and if his valor serves others, both he and they are blessed. But the glory of deeds is never free from pride; the joy beyond the joys of this world will be won by a valor beyond all human valor."

When Perceval was ready to leave, the abbot sent word for him to return to the chapel. The servants who had taken care of the knight's armor had been distressed by the condition of his shield, so worn it was nearly transparent. Hanging on the chapel wall was a fine white shield with a red cross on it. The abbot suggested that Perceval take it down. He did so, marveling at its lightness, and its strength that would withstand the heaviest blows. As he turned, with the shield in his hands, the abbot bowed low before him, thanking God that he had lived to see the knight of the grail. "The shield was left here for you many years ago by a maiden who said you would find it when you needed it. No other knight has been able to lift it from the wall."

Taking leave of the abbot, who gave him his blessing, Perceval rode down into a valley and then into a wasteland through which a lady came driving a cart covered in cloth of gold. She was an odd sight, for all her clothes were inside out, and she seemed to be lamenting bitterly as she whipped her horse to ever faster speed. The lady was so absorbed in her task that Perceval was close to her before she saw him, and she was startled by his greeting. When she turned to face him, however, all her troubles disappeared. "Thank God!" she cried. "I have found you at last! By the shield you bear I know you can defeat the devil himself!"

Perceval asked her what she meant, and why she was dressed that way. She was very willing to explain and told a terrible story. Deep within the Isles of the Sea, there was a great city, encircled with high stone walls and towers. It had been built by a powerful lord, later known as the Dragon Knight, and he had filled it with wicked folk, unbelievers who feared nothing. The knight himself had struck a bargain with the devil so that he would never be defeated in battle, and whenever he fought he wore the devil's own device, a huge jet-black shield, embossed with the head of a dragon that magically came to life in combat. Every man who challenged him was engulfed in flames from the dragon's mouth and died a horrible death. "That is how my dear love was murdered. The Dragon Knight is laying siege to Montesclaire, determined to wed the Lady of the Golden Circle, although she has sworn to kill herself before she lies with him. Of the five hundred knights who had gathered at the castle, my lover was one of the few who tried to rescue her, and it cost him his life. In my grief I swore to dress this way and display his body for all to see until he is avenged. That was more than two months ago. I have visited all the members of my lover's family, but no one has the courage to seek his killer. I know that only the bravest knight in the world could have set his hand to your shield. Will you help me?"

"I'll gladly do my best to avenge your friend."

"My lord, I will stay with you until the battle is over. May God grant you victory! Come with me now, I know the way very well. We will have to stop for the night at the Abbey of Saint Dominic, although we won't find much to eat there. The abbess and her people are starving, because almost all of their provisions come from Montesclaire. They have nothing but roots and wild apples."

The maiden turned her cart around, and the two of them set off. When they arrived at their destination, the abbess came out to greet them. The sight of the cross on Perceval's shield was so comforting to her that for the moment famine and fear were quite forgotten. Her nuns made haste to welcome Perceval and the lady, but they wept when they had to say there was nothing for them to eat, and only grass for the horses. They made their guests as comfortable as they could and spent the whole night praying for their safety.

A storm came up when Perceval and the lady set out the next morning, with so much thunder and lightning it seemed the earth would crack open. But soon the sun began to shine, and in a valley below them Perceval saw four packhorses, laden with food. These had broken free because of the noise and strong winds. Their owners were just catching up with them when Perceval arrived and asked if he could have something to eat. They invited him to join them in a meal and listen to some advice. "You must go back the way you came, my lord. This land belongs to a terrible tyrant, a man whose evil vices no book could describe. We are forced to serve him, and all we get is misery for our toil. He takes our wheat, oats, meat, and wine, and gives us nothing in return. He hates everyone who prays to God. Any knight he meets is burned to death by the flame-throwing dragon in his shield, a gift from the devil. That is why you must flee."

"I am sure what you say is true, but just the same I will try my strength against his. I'm glad to have something to eat first, since I have not had a meal for two days."

By this time the lady, whose name was Claire, had driven up in her cart and joined them. Although she was very hungry, she contented herself with bread and water, having vowed to fast until her lover was avenged. Perceval too ate moderately, as is wise before a battle. The horses had plentiful oats, which refreshed them greatly. Then Perceval and Claire continued their journey, she increasingly distressed as they approached their destination, fearing that Perceval would be killed. He, however, was eager to confront the Dragon Knight, whose encampment was soon visible right in front of the entrance to Montesclaire. It was positioned there to make sure no food was brought into the town, whose inhabitants were already weak from hunger. The Dragon Knight, who placed his faith in the devil, had demanded that they surrender to him their lady and her lands, or else they would all starve to death. Now it seemed that they had reached the end of their strength. Unless help arrived, they would have to yield the castle the very next day. The lady too had given up hope, although she knew that Gawain had vowed to rescue her, "and if only he had come, I would have been saved! Or the knight they call Perceval, who is searching for the grail." In her desperation she ran toward the windows of the hall, intending to end her agony, but the people of her household, who loved her very much, drew her back. Looking out from where she would have jumped, she saw a knight approaching. His shield was white with a red cross on it, and following him was a cart draped in gold brocade. The lady did not recognize the knight, but he seemed to her the handsomest in the world, and she thanked God for sending her a rescuer at last. "King Arthur's knights have done me no good at all, but this one will be different."

Meanwhile Perceval was looking at the Dragon Knight's army, spread over a vast plain. He noticed a tall tree with a huge bell hanging from its branches; four strong men would hardly be able to move its tongue an inch! Claire told Perceval that if he rang the bell, the whole army would come running, but they would do him no harm, being pledged to spare any knight who wanted to fight their lord.

Perceval did not hesitate. He went straight to the bellrope and pulled so hard that the countryside for miles around was filled with the clanging sound. Everyone rushed to the ramparts to see who had caused this great commotion; the lady of the castle and her attendants made their way to the high tower to have a better view.

Down below in his tent, the Dragon Knight began to prepare for battle, wondering aloud who had dared to sound the alarm. "It must be one of King Arthur's knights! He thinks he'll show how strong he is, but very soon he will die a horrible death!" Continuing to threaten his unknown challenger, he quickly donned his fighting gear and, slinging his shield around his neck, rode out to confront him.

As his enemy approached, Perceval sat his great Spanish warhorse and watched. His only response to the dragon was to raise his shield. The crimson cross shone on the white wood, and when the demon caught sight of it he was filled with terror and roared like a bull. The evil knight did not hesitate. Perceval lowered his lance and raced forward, but even before they met, his weapon was consumed by hellish fire and fell in cinders to the ground. The Dragon Knight fared no better; his lance shattered the moment it touched the cross. The noble horses had held so straight to their course that they collided head-on and were instantly killed. It was a great wonder that the two knights did not meet the same fate. The people of the castle gasped and then screamed as flames filled the air; they were sure that Perceval had died in the conflagration. But God wrought a miracle that day: so powerful was the red wood of the cross, that Perceval could not be harmed, and when the shields touched, the fire-breathing dragon was transformed into a crow and flew away with a shriek so ghastly that both knights fell senseless to the ground.

When the Dragon Knight regained consciousness, Perceval was already on his feet. His opponent grieved for the loss of his diabolical weapon, but Perceval wasn't displeased. They drew their swords and began to exchange such blows that the grass was red with blood. But when the Dragon Knight realized that he could not make a dent in the red and white shield, he hurled himself at Perceval, grabbing his wrists. Then his own forearms were seized in a mighty grip, and the two knights clung to each other so tightly that neither one could break free, letting go only long enough to land another hard blow. When they were finally so exhausted they fell to the ground, Perceval had the bad luck to lose hold of his sword. The Dragon Knight seized it and leaped to his feet. Perceval raised his shield and came at him, receiving a huge wound in his side, but managing to wrest the sword away.

The Dragon Knight shouted, "Your shield won't be enough to save you today!"

"We'll see about that!" was the reply. Then helmets were split and chain mail shredded, as the knights lunged, slashed, and hammered at each other. The Dragon Knight began to realize that his opponent seemed fresher than at the beginning of the battle. Drawing back, he said to him, "Were it not for your shield, you would have given up long since. It's not your skill or valor I am fighting, but some enchantment. If you are brave enough to face me without your shield, I promise to put mine down first. Then, if you beat me, the glory will be yours alone."

"As you wish!"

They placed their shields on the ground and fought with naked swords, giving each other such wounds it seemed no power on earth could heal them. When they were nearly at the end of their strength, Perceval's blade sliced right through the chain mail of the Dragon Knight's hauberk, cutting so deeply into the flesh that his entrails poured out. Desperate to sell his life dear, the Dragon Knight flung down his sword, rushed at his opponent, and fastened both arms tight around his waist. Perceval seized him in response, and the two men stood there, trying to crush each other. Then Perceval bent the Dragon Knight back until he collapsed on the ground. "Give up!"

"Never!"

"Ask for mercy!"

"I can't. No one can help me now."

"What would you give to be healed of your wounds?"

"Everything! My kingdom!"

"If you will do as I say, you'll be cured before sundown. I swear it."

"Tell me!"

"Send for the priest. Confess your wicked deeds and ask forgiveness for your sins! Your soul is even sicker than your body."

"You are right. I know I'm dying. Call the priest."

So it was that the Dragon Knight repented in the end and died absolved of all his sins.

The people of Montesclaire were beside themselves with joy, and as for their lady, she wept tears of happiness and relief, blessing the hour that Perceval had come their way. "You have saved me! I can never do enough to repay you, but I beg you to accept all my lands and wealth and myself with them. You deserve far more! But please have the soldiers bring food, for we are all dying of hunger!"

The enemy knights agreed to do everything Perceval asked; indeed, their lord had made them swear to obey any man who managed to defeat him. Food was quickly supplied—bread and wine and meats; there was plenty for everyone.

As the townsfolk made merry in the castle, the soldiers wrapped the Dragon Knight in a precious shroud and placed him on a litter. Perceval commanded them to take the body back to their own lands and bury their lord with honor. No sooner had they departed than Perceval himself made ready to leave. Mounted on the splendid horse the people of the castle had brought to him, he went to take leave of their lady. She pleaded with him to stay and let them do him honor, but he wanted to search for the lady Claire who had brought him to that place. It seemed that she had vanished.

He had traveled only a short distance when he saw her kneeling in his path. She said, "God be with you, noble knight! Thanks to your valor, my vow has been fulfilled. My love, who was burned to death, has had his vengeance. I must take him to the churchyard to be buried. Then I will go deep into the forest and find a place where I can live in solitude, praying for his soul and for my own, and especially for you, that God may grant you honor and joy, and lead you to your heart's desire."

"If that is His will," said Perceval, "and may your prayers be your salvation! Now I beg you to rise. It is not fitting for you to kneel before me."

Perceval took a path into the forest, and the lady went back to Montesclaire, where she saw her lover buried with great honor. Then she too went alone into the forest. She rode until she came to a brook running along the base of a mountainside. Nearby she found an abandoned hut which once had been a hermit's dwelling. There she stayed, living a life of devotion and great privation, in memory of her lost love. May God protect her and reward her for being so true! But now our story returns to Perceval.

*   *   *

AFTER LEAVING CLAIRE, he traveled through the forest all day until he came upon an old chapel. He tethered his horse, took off the bridle, and cut grass for him with his sword. In the chapel there was a statue of God's mother on the altar, and so it was to Mary that he prayed, asking her to preserve him from harm and guide him to the grail. Then, without removing his armor, he lay down beneath a pine tree.

No sooner had he closed his eyes than the devil tried to take him unawares. A most beautiful maiden came riding through the trees on a mule, and as she rode she lamented, "Oh, where is my dear love? When will I ever find him? I have been searching for so long!"

The knight woke up and raised his head. At that, the evil one jumped off her mule and cried, "Perceval, my beloved! For a whole year I have traveled the world looking for you everywhere! Now that I've found you at last, there is nothing I would not do for you! Why should you go on with this endless, painful quest when I myself can give you what you long for? I am the daughter of the Fisher King, and I love you with all my heart. Come lie here with me now, and everything you have ever desired will be yours."

"For shame!" said Perceval. "You may *look* noble and beautiful, but you are truly evil!" And he made the sign of the Cross. As the devil fled like a whirlwind screeching through the woods, every forest creature for miles around trembled with fear. Perceval drew his sword and made a circle around his horse and himself. Then he lay down and went peacefully to sleep.

*   *   *

WHILE ALL THESE EVENTS were taking place, Faradien and his wife had arrived at Carlion, where he declared himself King Arthur's prisoner. He related how he had been defeated by the knight who sought the grail, adding that he felt it no disgrace to have lost to one so valiant. Arthur made them welcome, and soon they were seated at dinner with many noble lords of the king's household. Just as the meal began, a squire was escorted to the king and fell on his knees before him. He explained that he was the messenger of a knight from beyond the sea, and that his master, whose armor was all of gold, was waiting in the meadow outside the castle, wanting to try his skills against the knights of the Round Table. King Arthur smiled at this news and called on Girflet, who hastened to arm himself and confront the challenger.

The entire court—king and queen, dukes, counts, knights, noble ladies and maidens—went out to watch, but what they saw was Girflet thrown to the ground, and then walking back toward them, head down, sick at heart. Sir Lancelot rode out to avenge Girflet, but that most worthy knight met the same fate, falling so heavily it was a long time before he could rise. No one could imagine how any knight could defeat the great Lancelot! But already Yvain and the unknown knight were hurtling toward each other; their stout lances struck at the same instant, and Yvain fell head over heels to the ground! In the next joust, when Sir Gawain rode out to defend the honor of Arthur's court, so powerful was the shock of the encounter that both horses crashed to the ground, leaving their riders senseless on the field. Then the opponents were on their feet, sword in hand, slashing through steel and chain mail. Gawain was furious when he could make no headway against a knight smaller than himself and who had jousted so much that day. The stranger seemed as fresh as he had been when he started!

A minstrel approached the king and said, "Sire, I know that knight! I recognize his armor. That is Tristan, who killed a dragon and won the fair Iseut for his uncle, King Mark of Cornwall. But magic made him fall in love with her, and she with him, and when the king found out about it, Tristan was banished from his lands."

At last King Arthur understood what was happening to his knights! His dismay gave way to delight, for Tristan's presence was an honor to his court. He hastened to put an end to the fighting and greet his noble guest. Gawain could not have been happier when he heard Tristan's name. The famous knight was welcomed by all, except for the ladies whose sweethearts had been publicly unhorsed!

At the king's urging, Tristan stayed at court for some time. It was soon apparent that the knight deserved his reputation. Not only was he a superb huntsman, he was also highly skilled at chess and backgammon and all the favorite diversions of the court. As a swordsman he was unbeatable, and it was just the same with hand-to-hand combat. Every knight who tried his luck was soundly defeated.

When Gawain saw how clever Tristan was, and how resourceful, he decided to challenge him to a wrestling match. The two friends met privately in Gawain's chambers where they could fight one another unobserved. Soon they were locked in combat, struggling and straining with all their might. Both were strong and powerful fighters, though Tristan was in fact the better of the two. Gawain, however, was quick, and with an unexpected movement of his knee, he caught Tristan off guard. Both men lost their balance and came crashing to the ground, with Tristan right on top of Gawain. He quickly jumped to his feet and, grinning at his friend, said, "Well, Sir Gawain, you win as usual!" Gawain got up, laughing, "If that's what you call being nearly crushed to death!" Off they went, joking and laughing about it. The two men became the best of friends, fighting together in tournaments and seeking adventure. But after a time, Tristan began to long for Iseut, and he asked the king's permission to go with ten or twelve other knights to visit King Mark's court. Arthur agreed, although he would have much preferred to keep Tristan with him.

Disguised as minstrels, they set out for Lancien, a powerful city where King Mark had challenged the King of the Hundred Knights to a tournament. They arrived in the evening when the day's fighting was over. There was feasting in the great hall, but everyone was somewhat subdued because their opponents had won all the prizes of that day. The king was sitting in state, Iseut beside him. With so many knights visiting the court, she could not help hoping that Tristan would be among them. It was well over a year since she had seen him last. A minstrel, wearing an ill-fitting scarlet cloak with holes in it, a strange round hat and a patch over one eye, his vielle slung around his neck, presented himself and his companions. In return for lodging, he said, "we are ready to entertain you." Iseut almost cried out when she heard his voice. How like Tristan's it was! But she couldn't recognize her beloved in the unkempt minstrel before her. The king said he would gladly listen to them. The knights in disguise tuned their instruments and began to play delightful melodies, to the great pleasure of all. The twelve companions were offered places at the table and served a fine meal.

Tristan could not take his eyes off Iseut. He was bitterly disappointed that she didn't recognize him, and determined to find a way to talk to her. Accompanying himself on his vielle, he began to sing "The Honeysuckle and the Hazel Tree":

> My love, we're like that vine and tree,
> I'll die without you, you without me.

This was a song that he and Iseut had written together to celebrate their love, and the queen was greatly distressed when she heard it. How could Tristan have taught their song to someone else? She looked more closely at the musician and finally understood: her lover was standing before her! There was not long to wait before the tables were taken away, and when Iseut retired for the night, she was not alone.

As the tournament continued, Arthur's knights saw that King Mark's side was unlikely to prevail. They decided to lend a hand and asked Iseut to provide them with horses and arms. The next morning they rode forth in great style, with freshly painted shields, good strong lances, and shining armor. Soon they were in the thick of it, driving back their opponents and knocking them to the ground. Their victims could not believe King Mark's knights were suddenly so impressive!

The tournament field was a vast plain bordered by a forest. Through these dense woods Perceval had been riding for many weeks. He was in a sorry state, his helmet badly dented and his shield full of holes, his hauberk red with rust. He urged on his horse, which was barely able to walk, and before long heard battle cries. He emerged from the forest close to the tournament field, where Sir Kay caught sight of him and, as usual, could not resist a disparaging remark. "The hero of the hour has arrived! That is a wonderful helmet you've got. It looks like chickens have been nesting in it!"

Perceval looked him up and down, and replied, "You ought to know! You must have learned your manners in a barnyard!"

He had scarcely finished speaking before Kay charged. Perceval's horse nearly collapsed under the impact, but Kay was flat on the ground. Perceval grabbed Kay's fresh horse and shouted, "Take mine! He'll teach you to ride!"

Kay's companions, Erec, Agravain, Cligès, and Bliobleris, galloped to his defense, but their horses were soon handed to their opponents. Now the odds were turning against King Mark, but Tristan would bring their un-

known assailant down! He galloped toward Perceval, leaning on his stirrups so hard he stretched the leather, determined to stop him from doing
more damage. But the soles of his boots were plain to behold as Perceval's
warped lance hurled him into the air. As the knight claimed his prisoner,
Lancelot, Yvain, Sagremor, and Gawain came racing toward him, sword in
hand. Perceval was ready and held his own against all four of them. After
a time, Gawain realized he had once before seen such prowess. He stopped
the fighting and said, "My lord, you were much better equipped when I last
saw you, but it doesn't make much difference to your style! I think I know
who you are, but please tell me your name."

"What is yours?"

"I am Gawain."

"And I am Perceval."

In the joy of their reunion, the tournament came to an end. Mark, who
was delighted by the prowess of King Arthur's knights, wanted to reward
them. They told him their only desire was that he be reconciled with Tristan
and welcome him back to court. Mark sighed, for he always feared that
Tristan might rob him of Iseut, but at last he agreed: "Dear nephew, from
now on, let us live together in peace."

That night when the prisoners on both sides had all been ransomed,
King Mark held a great feast in honor of Perceval. The next day he gave fine
horses and armor to Arthur's knights, who were setting out for home. They
told Perceval how much the king was longing to see him, but he said that
until he achieved the quest of the grail, he could not return to court. "But
tell King Arthur I greet him and pray that God will continue to grant him
honor, power, and joy."

With that he went his way and began again to roam the world, enduring
hunger and thirst and perilous adventures. Days turned into weeks, weeks
into months, and he began to wonder if his long search would ever come to
an end. One afternoon, exhausted by combat, he traveled through a terrible
storm, scarcely able to make his way against the wind-driven rain. The great
trees of the forest shrieked and groaned; panic-stricken beasts ran for cover.
But that night the moon rose clear and serene in a cloudless sky. Perceval
saw in the distance an enormous tree on which a thousand candles were
shining, bright as stars, twenty or thirty aflame on every branch. He hurried
as fast as he could, but the tree's brightness diminished as he approached. By
the time he arrived, there was only a faint glimmer emanating from a nearby

chapel. The light was coming through its open door. Perceval dismounted, left his horse to graze, and went inside.

No living thing was there, but on the altar lay the corpse of a knight, illuminated by a single candle. The body had been draped in a shroud of samite, richly hued and embroidered with golden flowers. Perceval, troubled and perplexed, was unable to tear himself from the eerie sight. All of a sudden the chapel blazed with white radiance as though a bolt of lightning were searing the air. When it vanished, the silence was shattered by a noise so appalling that Perceval thought the whole chapel was crashing in ruins around him. A hand, black to the elbow, slowly rose from behind the altar and, with a sudden gesture, snuffed out the light. The chapel was plunged into darkness.

Perceval had expected to find only holy things in such a place; what could this apparition mean? Since he had not been harmed, he imagined himself in no danger and was not afraid. But finding the darkness oppressive, he stayed no longer. He went to his horse and mounted, praying God to protect him from evil.

*   *   *

HE RODE ALL NIGHT, and when the mist rose with the sun, the castle he had feared he might never see again was there before his eyes! He had only to spur his horse and ride through its gate. Servants came running to greet him and see to his needs. When a fine cloak had been draped over his shoulders, he was accompanied through the great hall to a majestic chamber. Who could describe it? Nothing so splendid had been seen since the days of Judas Maccabeus. Silver stars shone in a ceiling of beaten gold and the walls were entirely covered with precious metals on which beautiful images had been engraved. Such a quantity of jewels adorned the walls that the air itself seemed to sparkle. Anyone would be struck with wonder at the sight.

The Fisher King welcomed Perceval graciously, giving him a place next to his own. He asked to hear about the previous day's adventures, and where Perceval had spent the night. Perceval recounted all that had happened: how he had come upon the chapel and found the dead knight on the altar, and how the black hand had appeared and put out the light. "My lord, I hope you can tell me what this means."

The king listened and, with a sigh, replied, "Thank God that you came to no harm! We will speak of this further, but now let us have something to eat. You are surely hungry after such a night."

They had not been long at table when a maiden, whiter than snow on winter branches, passed before them, holding the grail in her hand. A noble youth followed, carrying the lance; drops of blood ran from its tip to his hand. Next came another maiden of matchless beauty, dressed in white damask silk and carrying the silver carving dish. Perceval could wait no longer.

"Uncle, when I was here before, I truly wanted to ask about the grail, but I was afraid you would find me too bold. A holy hermit told me that was because I lacked God's favor. Now I hope that my long journey has atoned for my failure, and that you will speak to me of these wonders, and tell me who is served by the grail, and what the bleeding lance means."

The Fisher King replied, "Knowledge of the grail is not like knowledge of other things. The grail's radiance lies within your own soul, but it has no meaning that can be said in words. The grail is the source of all true valor, a sign of God's presence on earth. It brings to the old king a single holy wafer, and this is all he has eaten for twelve years. He never leaves his room, his life sustained and made joyful by the grail.

"The drops of blood that flow from the lance remind us that the result of violence is inevitably pain. Woe to the knight who uses his power only for his own ends, no matter how noble these may seem! That is is how I received the wound that has made me an invalid. When I had succeeded my father here at Corbenic, my brother was treacherously killed by Partinal. Seeking revenge, I challenged him, and we fought for long hours. Finally I had him on the ground, my sword at his throat. When he said he would rather die than beg for mercy, I did not hesitate to strike the fatal blow. But my lack of compassion was instantly punished. As I turned away, I slipped on the blood-soaked ground and fell against the sword that had dropped from his hand. The wound I received has never healed.

"Because of my sin, a never-ending punishment has been inflicted on my lands and my people. The hand of darkness reaches out into our world, appearing at will in every church and chapel of my kingdom, slaying any knight who enters. That you were spared is a great wonder and brings me hope. In the shadow of that hand, crops wither and die, animals do not give birth, and women bear no children. I live here with my father and our few faithful servants, safe in the protection of the grail, but my people live in fear and desperate need. I can do nothing to help them; we can only wait for the knight who will vanquish this evil, releasing my kingdom from the blight. If that is your destiny, you will find yourself again in the chapel where the Black Hand destroys knights, and this time you will confront it. What follows is yet to be revealed."

The Fisher King would say no more. He and his guest soon retired for the night. Perceval slept fitfully and was up at break of day; he was eager to set out, for he now had a new sense of his mission. After saying his prayers, he rode into the forest. He traveled through many lands, where his presence was a blessing to innocent people in need of help, a grief to their enemies. Finally he found himself traveling toward his homeland and came to the Valbone Pass, in the remote forest that encircles the mountain there. He knew the place well; nearby he had seen knights for the first time, and believed that they were angels.

He rode on, lost in thought, until the forest came to an end. Across a plain there was a stone castle with crenelated walls. A palisade of untrimmed oak logs protected its bridge. Perceval urged on his horse, for soon it would be dark. He saw five knights riding ahead of him, their horses clearly exhausted. The knights were armed, but all their gear was worn and broken, scarcely a hand's breadth of metal intact in their helmets and golden shields, their swords notched and twisted. They had all been badly wounded, but one was close to death. Four spears had torn through his body, and his head was split open to the skull. The others supported him, riding along as slowly as they could, lamenting bitterly. The land around the castle had been laid waste; no farms or dwellings were to be seen. Perceval greeted the knights, and one of them very courteously replied, "May God in his majesty preserve you from harm, and bring you to great joy."

"I thank you for that, my lord, and hope you will tell me what has happened to you and your companions."

"Ah, my lord, no one has ever endured such misfortune! I will tell you all about it, but we need to get our father home as quickly as we can. Come with us now, and stay the night. It's a long ride to the next dwelling."

Perceval thanked him. Soon they were inside the castle gates. The desperately wounded knight was carried into the hall, where a bed had been prepared by the fire. As they removed his armor and tended to his wounds, Perceval heard one of the men sigh, "I'm afraid that this time he won't recover." The sons were far more concerned with their father's injuries than their own, but they took pains to hide their distress and show fitting hospitality to their guest. After a time, the lord of the manor spoke: "My sons, I hope you will honor our guest. He reminds me of the young Welsh fellow I made a knight some years ago."

Perceval realized with a start that his host was none other than Gornemant, his old teacher. "My lord, it breaks my heart to see you like this! Tell me who your enemies are and where I can find them. I owe you everything!"

Gornemant, with great effort, raised himself on one elbow, "Hear, then, the terrible suffering we have endured, and will endure, until this castle has been destroyed, and my life with it. Every morning forty knights, fine warriors, ride up to my gate on tall swift horses. Every day we have to fight them, I and my four sons, for we are all that is left of my household. Our foes are fierce and powerful, but by evening they all lie dead on the field. And then in the night they come alive again, though we have never dared to stay and see how that happens. The next morning they are back, just as before, and we must do battle with them all over again. Now I am so badly wounded that tomorrow my sons will have to fight without me, only the four of them against forty strong knights."

"My lord," said Perceval, "I will be with them tomorrow in your place, and hope to repay your great kindness to me when I was so young and ignorant."

Gornemant thanked him, and soon they all retired for the night, but Perceval, preoccupied by thoughts of his host's suffering, scarcely slept. He prayed that God would help him to deliver Gornemant from his foes.

At daybreak the household began to stir; already the forty knights stood waiting. Perceval's armor was spread before him on a silk cloth, and servants hurried to help him prepare for battle. A solemn mass was sung, and then the four knights took leave of their father.

"God be with you, my sons! May He keep you safe and bring you back to me!"

The horses had been brought to the chapel door. As they mounted, Perceval called out to his companions that they should take some nourishment before fighting. Servants brought silver goblets full of wine into which the knights dipped bread. Then they laced their helmets firmly, the gates were opened, and the five rode out to confront the enemy knights who were drawn up in battle formation in a field some distance away.

At the sight of the small group of their opponents, the forty knights charged as one. Perceval brandished his lance and galloped forward. He struck through the shield of the first knight he met, tearing open his chest. Commending the dead man to all the devils of hell, he plunged his lance into a second knight, flinging him from his horse. His soul left his body before he hit the ground. But there were thirty-eight warriors left! Perceval killed eight before his lance finally shattered, taking so many blows himself that his shield was in pieces. The air rang with the sound of metal on metal as his adversaries hammered away at him, like blacksmiths pounding an anvil! Wild with fury, Perceval drew his sword and instantly cut off the head of his nearest assailant. The four brothers were right behind him; wounded though they were, they did their best to help, wielding mighty blows but receiving many more. Soon their shields were in tatters, all their armor dented and full of cracks. Suddenly one of the brothers fell, as a sword slashed into his head. The others dragged him to a sheltered place but soon were back in the fray, battling on until only twenty of the enemy were left. They paused for a few moments to draw breath but made haste to follow Perceval as he returned to the attack. Inspired by his courage, they fought with great spirit, harder than ever. But finally all three of them were brought down with wounds so huge that their entrails were spilling out. The four enemy knights who were still alive thought they would make quick work of Perceval. He beheaded one and split the skull of another; but the third one cried out, "You have worked for nothing, Perceval! Before you wake up tomorrrow, we will all be here waiting for you!"

"You'll come at your peril," said Perceval, "but whatever happens tomorrow, today you will join your friends!"

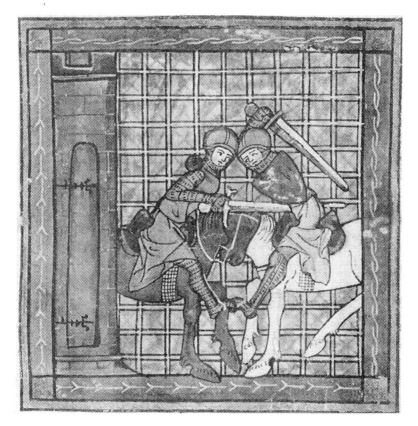

The knight charged, shouting, "You can't frighten us with death!" as
Perceval cut through his neck. The last knight had his shoulder sliced off
and dropped like a stone from his horse.

The forty knights lay dead. Perceval went to help his companions, binding up their wounds and doing them so much good that they were able to
get on their horses, despite their pain. They said to him, "My lord, come
home with us now and have some rest for the night. Tomorrow you can be
on your way again. As for us, we won't live to see noon, and even if we did,
we would have to fight these knights all over again, and there is no way we
could do that. They have sworn to destroy us all and burn our castle to the
ground. That is what awaits us tomorrow."

"God forbid! You must go now, but I intend to stay here and find out
how those knights come back to life. I won't leave this place until I know the
truth!"

Nothing the brothers said could dissuade him. They rode sadly back to their castle, where they told Gornemant how Perceval had saved them from certain death, and now would die himself, "the bravest and most generous knight in the world!" They were all overcome with grief and spent the night lamenting the loss of their friend.

He, meanwhile, had been sitting on an outcropping of rock above the battlefield, holding his horse by the bridle. After a time he began to shiver with cold and decided to move about. Thus he passed the hours until after midnight, when a rising moon illuminated the scene. Perceval, gladdened by this, sat down again to keep watch. Along one side of the field was a stone wall in which he saw a door begin to open. Perceval crossed himself as a tall old woman appeared, carrying two wonderfully wrought ivory casks, ringed with bands of solid gold and encrusted with precious stones, so valuable that King Arthur, with all his riches, could not have bought them.

The old woman who carried the casks was ugly beyond all imagining. She was scrawny and dry as an old stick, her skin the color of smoke. One of her eyes was small and red, the other immense and black; they were set askew in her ghastly, hairy face. Two braids, like rat tails, flapped against her neck. Her torso was hunched and gnarled, her gait so unsteady it seemed she would fall down at every step.

"God in heaven," thought Perceval, "how can she be so hideous? Is it some evil enchantment, or did she crawl straight out of hell?"

But Perceval was no coward. Wanting to know what the hag was going to do, he kept quiet and didn't move. He watched her limp toward the dead warriors strewn about the field. She set the casks down and, bending over a body, took hold of the severed head and joined it to the neck. Then she removed the stopper from one of the casks. Perceval was watching her every move.

The old woman poured into her palm a single drop of liquid, clearer than rose water. She touched the drop with her finger and rubbed it over the dead man's lips. Suddenly, every wound was healed, every vein and joint in his body was filled with life! Before you could count to three, he was back on his feet. This must have been the balm that anointed our Lord! The crone restored four others in the same way as the first; then she rubbed the mouth of another, and he too sprang up. Perceval, horrified, could wait no longer. He leaped onto his horse and, brandishing his sword, galloped up to the crone and shouted: "Whatever you have done for them, your potion won't do *you* any good!"

The old woman looked at him in astonishment and rage. "Perceval! No one of your lineage has ever possessed a treasure as great as this! But you will have to fight for it!"

"So be it! But tell me who these men are, and why they are attacking Gornemant."

"Gornemant made you a knight, and for this he must be destroyed. Without him, you would never have seen the grail. While I am alive, you will not see it again!"

As she bent down to anoint another of the dead, Perceval raised his sword and, with one swift blow, cut off her head. Instantly he was attacked by the six knights she had restored. His horse was killed under him, and he suffered many wounds, but he stood his ground until he alone was left alive on the field. At last, he sat down to rest, leaning against his dead horse. He still gripped his sword, the blade bright as ice and dripping with blood. After a time, he went over to look at the casks. Their beauty was extraordinary, but their power was even more compelling. "Could it really be true?" he wondered. "Could I myself restore the dead to life?" Perceval moistened his finger with a drop of the balm, and touched the mouth of the warrior nearest him, who at once sprang to his feet and struck a blow that cut through the knight's helmet. "A curse on anyone who helps you again!" cried Perceval, returning the warrior's attack with such fury that his life's blood spilled to the ground. Then Perceval, thinking he could at least do some good for himself, touched a drop of the balm to his own lips, and his wounds were healed completely. He would not have exchanged that medicine for the whole world! He put the stoppers, two large rubies, into the casks which sparkled with emeralds and sapphires. Overjoyed with his treasure, and impatient to see the dawn, he sat there waiting.

Gornemant, unable to sleep, was grieving for Perceval, and lamenting the fate that would now overtake them all. His sad thoughts were interrupted by a maiden who came rushing in to say she had heard Perceval calling from outside! Gornemant was so happy that he ran all the way to the drawbridge, completely forgetting his wounds. When he asked why the knight was on foot, Perceval explained that his horse had been killed, "but I've gained much more than I lost!" He told all about the old woman, how wicked and ugly she was, and how she brought the dead back to life.

In the hall were Gornemant's sons, lying in beds. They were in such pain that they kept losing consciousness, but they were happy to see Perceval alive. He placed a drop of the magic balm on the lips of each one, and they were all as well as the fishes in the sea. If God had come down from the sky, he could not have been embraced more heartily than Perceval! They rejoiced together, and Gornemant and his sons hoped that the knight would stay with them for a long time. He, however, wanted to leave the very next morning for Beaurepaire and asked Gornemant to accompany him, "because, if you will agree, I wish to make your niece Blanchefleur my wife. I rescued her when her castle was under siege, and we fell in love. I said then that she would be my wife, but for all these years I've been searching for the grail, and my quest has prevented me from keeping my promise."

Gornemant replied, "Nothing could make me happier than this marriage. Of course I will go with you, gladly, and do you every honor that I can."

They spent the whole day in great contentment, talking of only the happiest things and eating sumptuous meals. When at last they were ready to sleep, the servants prepared a bed for Perceval in a room whose paneled walls were ornamented with gold. He slept under silk and fur, while Gornemant and his sons had their own beds set close by in case he needed anything. To the sound of a Cornish flute, a minstrel softly sang "The Lay of Guiron," and soon they were fast asleep. Perceval woke up during the night and saw the whole room glowing with light from the ivory casks. He felt no fear but only wonder at that sign of their holiness. Then he slept soundly until the watchman's horn greeted the dawn, but even after he awoke he lay in bed, tired from all his exertions; it had been a long time since he'd slept in such comfort. When the bell rang for mass, he dressed quickly and joined the others.

After the service, Perceval wanted to leave immediately for Beaurepaire, but Gornemant, though pleased by this eagerness, persuaded him to wait until after breakfast. Soon they were mounted and on their way, Perceval riding a fine swift horse, a gift from Gornemant. The older man carried the ivory casks himself. They rode very fast and before long were within sight of Beaurepaire. Gornemant had not seen Beaurepaire since it had been laid waste by Clamadeus, and was amazed by the prosperity of the city. Ships were arriving there by sea and on the Humber River, and they brought goods from many lands, assuring constant and lively trade. There were meadows, orchards, farmlands, and vineyards, and beyond these stretched the forest, full of game.

Perceval sent two young men ahead to tell Blanchefleur he had come.

They galloped off and made their way through crowds of people. When at last they reached the palace, they found the maiden beautifully attired in pure white silk, seated among the members of her household. But when they drew near, the messengers were so overwhelmed by her loveliness they could not utter a single word. Blanchefleur was thinking of how long it had been since she had seen Perceval. "Alas, if he loved me the way I love him, he would be here now! But no matter what anyone says, I will never give up hope! If I have to, I'll wait for him forever."

By now the two messengers had recovered their nerve and their voices. Kneeling in front of Blanchefleur, they said, "Lady, your friend, the valiant Perceval, sends you his greetings."

At these words, she nearly fainted. When she understood that Perceval was on his way to see her, and Gornemant too, she was so overcome with joy that she leaped to her feet, and would have run all alone through the streets to meet him, had her ladies not pulled her back, reproaching her for behaving so wildly. "Let go of me!" she said. "If you had ever been in love, you would understand!" At last she agreed to do as they said and had her people prepare elegant garments fit for a prince or a king. Silk and samite were draped from all the windows of the town, and the streets lined with rich carpets. It looked like an earthly paradise! The lists were prepared for jousting and the horses caparisoned in finest silk. Amidst great rejoicing, Blanchefleur set out on a palfrey decked in gold brocade and glittering with jewels. A magnificent procession of knights and ladies followed. Blanchefleur wore a crimson cloak lined with ermine, and everyone who saw her was enchanted. Her beauty was truly beyond the power of words.

When she caught sight of Perceval riding toward her, she stopped, blushing deeply, scarcely able to return his ardent greeting, "my beloved!" She gazed at him with longing and softly murmured, "my dearest love." But instantly they were surrounded by people welcoming the knight who had saved them from disaster. Singing and dancing, they led him through the gates of the city and all the way to the palace where clarions were announcing that a feast had been prepared. And it was truly worthy of the occasion! Not only were all the knights and ladies royally served, but there were no guards at the doors, and anyone could come in and take as much of the food and drink, and also candles, as he desired. That night it looked as if the town had been set on fire!

When dinner was over, Perceval rose to his feet and spoke to Blanchefleur's vassals: "My lords, I have come to ask your lady to be my wife. If she will have me, and if you agree, we will send for the priest right away."

They replied, "When you and our lady are married, my lord, we will never know sadness again."

"Then let it be tomorrow."

The maiden sighed for joy. No man who ever lived could compare to her Perceval!

After a very happy evening, Blanchefleur's guests were shown to a magnificent chamber hung with tapestries and decorated with gold and enamels, where five beds were set up for Gornemant and his sons. Perceval's bed, on the other side of the room, was covered with a cloth of wondrous hue, more speckled than the feathers of a goshawk. A magic spell had been woven into the silk, so that no one who lay under it could come to any harm.

In another richly appointed chamber, Blanchefleur and the ladies of her household had retired for the night; soon all but Blanchefleur were fast asleep. Thoughts of love kept her awake, and before long she began to debate with herself: "Shall I go see him? No, I dare not! Surely he'd love me less if I were so brazen! But I've always gone to visit him! He will think I've become proud, now that I know we're to be married. He may reproach me, but I have to go!"

She sat up and reached for her shift and cloak. Emboldened by love, she made her way to Perceval's bed. He heard her coming, and stretched out his arms to draw her under the covers. There they lay, entwined in one another's arms, sharing sweet kisses and murmuring tender words. They went no further, for they wished to enjoy the fullness of love when they had been honorably married. At the first glimmer of dawn, Blanchefleur returned to her own bed, and there she remained until the sun was up and light filled the room. Soon the sounds of jousting could be heard, and of laughter and merriment. All the ladies of the city were wearing their finest clothes, and the seneschal passed among them, encouraging everyone to have a wonderful time.

Perceval rose from his bed and quickly dressed. How handsome he was with his curly blond hair, gray eyes, straight nose, and cleft chin! A small scar on his forehead only added to his good looks. From his broad shoulders draped in scarlet silk, to his long, well-formed legs, he was the image of knightly perfection.

Blanchefleur, of course, was also up and about. Her ladies dressed her in bright red, trimmed with burnished gold and gems that sparkled like fire. Over her shoulders they draped a magnificent scarlet cloak lined with white ermine fur.

The common folk were already gathering before the great hall, the sounds of their merrymaking heard far and wide. Everyone began to move toward the church, where the archbishop of Landemeure had come to conduct the marriage service. Many other clergymen were present, as eager as everyone else to see Perceval, who now came riding toward them, with Blanchefleur beside him. Their joy made them more beautiful than ever, and people hastened to the church to have a better view. Perceval stopped in front of the main portal, dismounted, ran to Blanchefleur, and lifted her to the ground. Gornemant was ready to escort his niece to the altar, where the archbishop took the two young people by the hand. Soon he had joined them in lawful matrimony.

Great was the rejoicing in Beaurepaire as the crowds made their way back to the palace. Jongleurs were playing melodies on their vielles and singing songs of love. Everyone sat down to eat a dinner elegantly served from great silver platters. Then minstrels played music for dancing, while storytellers told beautiful tales for those who preferred to sit and listen. When the entertainers had finished, they were lavishly praised and rewarded with fine clothing and purses full of gold. Those who arrived poor went home wealthy!

Nightfall came, and still the revelry went on. While supper was being served in the brightly lit hall, maidservants were busy preparing the nuptial bed in Blanchefleur's chamber. When all was ready, the archbishop and high clergymen came to bestow their blessing. Everyone was eager to do the noble lady honor, for her lands were richer than any others, save those of King Arthur himself. And of all her great wealth, and of her own person, she had made Perceval lord. When the time came, the new husband and wife went to bed, and the company at last dispersed. Blanchefleur's maids had no qualms about leaving her alone with Perceval; they knew she would be even happier tomorrow!

Trembling with desire, they lay in one another's arms. Perceval pressed Blanchefleur to him, and she, who was in every way a perfect and noble lady, said, "My love, let us be careful what we do this night. The devil is only too ready to take us unawares."

The very power of their yearning held them back, for they wished to do nothing that might be displeasing to God. With one accord, they rose and knelt together in prayer, asking God to grant them the gift of abstinence. Then they returned to bed and, holding one another in a loving embrace, at once fell peacefully asleep. At daybreak, Perceval awoke. There was a radiance in the room, and he heard a voice saying, "Perceval, remember that the one you have wed is full of goodness, and that a man must always touch his wife respectfully, and never lie with her just to satisfy carnal lust. Trust in God, be compassionate, and great honor will be yours. From your line will be born a maiden, beautiful and gracious; she will marry a rich king, and bear three sons. Your great-grandsons will take back Jerusalem and the Holy Sepulcher. But Perceval, your quest is not yet complete. You must depart once more or lose all honor in the world, for yourself and your descendants. More than this, I cannot say. I commend you to God." With these words, the voice was still and the light vanished.

Perceval lay awake for a long time, thinking of what had been said to him. When it was time to get up, squires came to help him dress, and Blanchefleur's attendants were ready with elegant clothes for her too. After mass, Blanchefleur's vassals paid homage to Perceval as their new lord. But Perceval told them he must soon depart, and that Gornemant was to rule in his behalf and be the protector of his wife and of his lands. They must be as loyal to him as to Perceval himself, "for I must set out again. My quest is not yet accomplished and I can stay with you no longer." He asked that his armor and his horse be made ready at once.

Blanchefleur was heartbroken when she learned that Perceval was leaving. She had thought that if he came back and made her his wife, he would stay with her forever. But having once seen his extraordinary courage, she could never object to anything he wanted to say or do. She loved him so dearly that no matter how long he stayed away, her love would be undiminished. So Perceval took his leave, sadly but in peace, and once again rode away into the forest.

*　　*　　*

FOR TWO DAYS he neither ate nor slept, nor did he see any sign of human life. But as the trees gradually became more widely spaced, sunlight began to filter through and at last the forest came to an end. When he emerged into

the open, he saw the great tower of a castle not very far away. Its windows
and crenelations displayed an impressive array of shields. Perceval rode
through the main gate and into a courtyard where he found a lady with a
small child, accompanied by twenty knights. Since the day was very hot, she
was dressed in a simple shift. Perceval dismounted and greeted her courteously. "You are welcome here, my lord," she said, "though you will have to
follow the custom of this house. I pray you will come to no harm." She said
no more about it, but she and the knights seemed glad to escort Perceval
indoors, and he was well content to find lodging there. They helped him
off with his armor and brought him a fresh change of clothes. Then the
lady led him to the great hall where he was surprised to see a magnificent
ivory casket, adorned with gold and silver bands, and precious jewels that
glittered in the light of many candles. A golden key was hanging next to
the lock.

Sure that such a casket must contain holy relics, Perceval asked his hostess who the saint might be. "No one knows," she replied. "Some years ago a swan came to these shores, pulling a boat by a silver chain. My lord and his brothers heard a piercing cry and ran down to the sea. There they found the boat, and on it this casket, along with a letter written in a fine hand, which instructed them to carry the casket into the hall and accord it every honor. It said further that the casket could only be unlocked by the greatest knight in the world, and opening it would show how their father died. My lord and his brothers have never stopped grieving for their father, who set out for King Arthur's court and never returned. This is why they constantly search the forest paths and the seven royal roads, capturing any knight they find and making him try the lock. A hundred have tried, but in vain. The last one was Sir Gawain, who put up a great fight. He injured several of the men before he would agree to do as they required. When he, too, failed, my lord locked him away with all the others. Now I have told you everything I know, and may God protect you."

Perceval thanked her, though he was distressed to learn of Gawain's plight. Suddenly there was a commotion at the door as the lord, his brothers, and their companions arrived. Squires rushed out to take the horses, but Perceval stayed where he was. The men came in fully armed, swords at their sides, lances in hand, helmets laced on. The lady's husband, whose name was Leander, stepped forward, his three brothers close behind him. They were powerful warriors who feared no one. Wasting no word of greeting on Perceval, Leander demanded that he try to open the casket then and there.

"Your wife told me of this custom, and I have no objection."

Perceval went straight to the casket. He would have done better to refuse! He took the key and put it in the lock. The four brothers and their friends stood at his back. With one turn of the key, the lock snapped open. Perceval raised the lid. People crowded around to see what was inside. A musky scent, like that of incense, filled the room. Leander looked in and saw a body, draped in richly embroidered cloth, with its right arm exposed. In the hand was a sheet of parchment covered with golden letters. He took it and asked that the message be read aloud. Everyone there heard these words: "Look at my face and you will know who I am. The one who opened the casket murdered me."

Leander drew back the silk shroud and stared intently at the half-ruined face. A javelin blow through the eye had pierced the brain. Suddenly he realized who was lying in the coffin. "Oh, God!" he cried, "it's our father!" The brothers stared at each other in stunned silence. At last Leander spoke. "Father has shown us his fate, and bequeathed to us his vengeance. But even a hundred deaths would not compensate for his."

As Perceval stood there among the grief-stricken sons, he thought to himself that God must surely desire his death. "I'll never escape. There is no way to reach my weapons." The brothers were just about to cut him down, when he caught sight of an axe hanging on the wall. With one swift move he seized it and instantly snatched the young child from his mother's arms. Turning to confront them all, he said, "If you really want my life, it will cost you dear!"

"You'll never get away with it!" shouted Leander. "You murdered our father in cold blood! I'll have you drawn and quartered like the coward you are!"

"It is true that I killed your father, but he attacked me first! I was young and foolish and believed Sir Kay when he said I could have the Red Knight's armor. I had none of my own. Your father became so angry that he swung his lance and struck me a vicious blow. Before I knew it, my javelin had gone right through his eye. Surely you understand that it wasn't my fault. If you try to kill me, I will use the boy as my shield. I would hate to see him die."

With a heart-rending cry, the mother fell to her knees, imploring her husband to have mercy. Leander was nearly out of his mind with grief and rage. To reach his enemy, he would have to harm his son, and he would rather die than do that. He had his men draw back and said to Perceval, "I will offer you a bargain to your advantage. Take all the time you need to arm yourself. There are four of us brothers. You must fight me first, and if you win, you must fight each of the others. If you defeat us all, you shall go free, and our prisoners with you."

Perceval replied, "I accept your terms. Bring me my arms; I would rather fight than be killed."

Leander had the armor and weapons brought into the courtyard. Perceval put down the child and ran to his waiting horse. Then he made haste to get ready, shortening his stirrups to keep his seat more firmly. He mounted, laced his helmet, and took up a lance with a heavy metal tip. Leander, eager for battle, was already astride a powerful, swift-running warhorse. He swore he would give up all rights to his own lands if he didn't slaughter Perceval like a helpless sheep.

Perceval, seeing Leander so proud, so wild with rage, prayed to God: "Forgive my shortcomings, Lord, and protect me in this fight."

Then they charged, their horses passing so close together that the lances penetrated the shields and tore through the hauberks. Both knights felt cold steel graze their ribs. The points lodged in the cantles of the saddles, but the horses galloped straight on, exploding the lances into a thousand pieces. Both men were stunned by the impact; their horses staggered beneath them and crashed to the ground, the riders still clinging to their necks. The knights struggled to their feet, unsheathed their swords, and struck. Soon their shields and helmets were in pieces, and chain mail links were flying through the air. Blood and sweat stained their faces; their eyes burned from the dust. For an instant they both stood back, but their rage would not let them rest. They grasped their shields and came together again, each one raining blows on the other's head. Blood poured from their wounds, reddening the grass. Leander looked at his wife, her pale sweet face wet with tears. He lunged at Perceval in such murderous fury that his blade tore through the hauberk into the flesh, right to the bone. The heavy blade swung down to the ground, snapping off the point of Perceval's spur. He was very lucky not to have lost his foot.

Leander saw him stagger. "You're finished!" he said. "Now you will answer for my father's death."

"We're not through yet," Perceval replied. "We aren't fighting about your father any more. It's you who will answer to me for the blood you have spilled today."

But he knew he must defeat Leander soon, or he would have no strength left for the other three. He attacked with such ferocity that Leander was forced to retreat. As he fled, he stumbled to his knees. His wife shrieked aloud. With renewed determination, Leander rose to confront his opponent once again. Neither prevailed until nightfall, when at last Perceval struck Leander down, right at the feet of his wife.

"I beg you, my lords, fight no more today," she entreated. "There will be time enough tomorrow."

Perceval replied, "I would rather end this now. Why not make peace? You have little to gain by my death."

But Leander said, "Never! Not as long as I live!"

"That is a great pity," said Perceval. "May God show me a way to gain your friendship."

A truce was made for the night and Leander had everyone leave the field of battle. Drenched in sweat and blood, he disarmed in the great hall by candlelight. His brothers gently cleaned and bandaged the wounds. Everyone was horrified to see how badly he had been injured. Meanwhile, the lady Ysmaine led Perceval to an elegant bedchamber and helped him off with his armor. Her husband, whom she loved deeply, had made her promise to take care of the knight as best she could, forgetting for the moment the enmity between them. She carefully removed his shirt and wiped the blood from the deep wound in his side. A woman named Elie helped her draw the edges together with a cotton cloth soaked in balm, and wrap a silk bandage firmly around his chest. Then they draped a new fur-trimmed cloak about his shoulders. Four servants entered the room, two of them carrying lighted torches, the others setting up a table and bringing in food. A young maiden also came, at the lady's request, and helped her keep Perceval company. Ysmaine said, "Sir, we will take good care of you tonight, and tomorrow your horse and equipment will be returned. I cannot answer for what may happen to you after that. God grant that you and my husband make peace, and that he pardon you for his father's death."

"God hear you, lady, and may he grant you every joy."

"Please do me the honor of dining with me. There will be shad, perch, and salmon, with spiced wine to drink. I hope you will enjoy it."

After dinner, they prepared a soft bed for him. His weapons were placed on a table close by, and the lady had two lamps lighted, so that he could see to arm himself if he had to. Perceval lay quietly and listened to a minstrel

sing a tale of marvelous adventure. Though he was surrounded by enemies, the knight gave no sign of being afraid. Ysmaine waited until he
was asleep and quietly left the room. The minstrel bolted the door behind
her. She went back to the hall where she found her husband sitting with his
brothers and other members of the household. The ointment they had put
on his wounds had made him feel much better. She served him a nourish-
ing oxtail soup and then took precious spices that she carried in a little
purse, cinnamon, nutmeg, cloves, and bright red pomegranate seeds, and
had them ground together in a mortar. These were mixed with hot wine to
relieve his dizziness. He would be completely cured in three days, if only
he did not insist on fighting tomorrow. Then they retired for the night.
Leander's brothers stayed up for a while talking about the fight. Evander
said that the knight had not only held out against Leander but seemed to
get stronger as the day wore on. "If he can defeat Leander, the rest of us
don't have a chance." They all agreed that it would be better to settle the
dispute, if they could do so honorably, without further bloodshed. At
that, they went to sleep.

Meanwhile, in another part of the castle, four other brothers were having a quite different conversation. These were Leander's close relatives, but
he hated them for having convinced his father to demand King Arthur's
lands. He would never have done so otherwise. Wanting to get back in their
cousin's good graces, the four decided to kill Perceval as he lay sleeping. If
they avenged the Red Knight's death, Leander would surely be grateful.
They took up flaming torches, seized their weapons, and went down the
stairs of the tower where they were lodged. The minstrel jumped from his
bed at the sound of an axe crashing into the door. "My lord, wake up!" he
cried. "We're being attacked! Leander has been betrayed, but I will defend
you to the death!" Perceval leaped from his bed and armed himself as best
he could. The minstrel found a good helmet in the room and asked Perceval
to help him lace it on. He also grabbed an axe and an old shield. The knight
ran to the door shouting, "Cowards! You thought you could take me by
surprise! You'll pay for your mistake." Then he drew back the bolt and
flung the door wide open. One of the attackers was right in front of him,
shield held high. He thought that the wounded man would be an easy prey,
but Perceval did not hesitate, hitting him such a blow that the shield split in
two and he fell crashing down the stairs. The three others pushed their way
into the room and surrounded Perceval, wielding their swords. The minstrel

was swinging his axe so valiantly that the two of them would have carried the day, had the first assailant not reappeared. Perceval was sorely pressed, but as the odds against him increased, so did his strength. The minstrel too was fighting like one possessed. He swung his axe, splitting the helmet of an attacker, but just then he lost his grip, and the man was saved from death. The axe crashed to the flagstone floor and broke. The traitor, seeing his chance, brought down his sword on the minstrel's shoulder, severing tendons and bone. But almost before the defenseless minstrel fell dead, Perceval's sword had slashed through his killer's neck, flooding the stone floor with blood. "Cut him down!" screamed one of the brothers. "He can't get away with this!"

"Traitors!" cried Perceval. "You'll never win!"

He hurled himself at the closest of them, and the man collapsed to his knees, blood gushing from his nose. His brothers, enraged, redoubled their efforts, to no avail. Perceval would have defeated them both, but four of their servants, wielding axes, suddenly joined in. Now the noise in the room became so great that Ysmaine, in her distant chamber, realized that Perceval was under attack. She awakened Leander, who leaped to his feet, calling out to his brothers, "Get up! Our guest is being murdered!"

The brothers seized their weapons, the servants took up torches, and they all rushed from the room. By now the whole household was awake, and everyone was shouting at Leander, "How could you break the truce! Are you mad?"

"The truce has been broken, but not by me! Help us now, or leave my house forever!"

Leander ran on ahead. There was Perceval, still valiantly defending himself. He had already killed three of his eight assailants. At the sight of Leander he lost heart; his strength could not prevail against so many. But when he heard Leander shouting, "Foul murderers! How dare you break my truce! You'll die for this!" he realized that the minstrel was right, and the brothers had not betrayed him. These came running with other members of the household; the traitors were seized and tightly bound. Leander swore that in the morning they would get what they deserved. His brother Marmadus shouted, "They killed the minstrel and attacked the knight who was under our protection. Make them pay for that, or we will live in shame!" Leander's wife and Meliadus also urged Leander to do justice. The traitors were locked in a tower to wait for morning.

As they talked, Ysmaine was binding up Perceval's wounds, after carefully treating them with a soothing ointment. Then she put him to bed. Leander came in and said the truce would be extended until Perceval was completely restored to health. Perceval replied, "Your truce has been worth very little up to now. If it hadn't been for the minstrel they would have murdered me in my sleep. And he wielded his axe like a warrior! May his killers get what they deserve!" Leander assured him that he need not worry.

The next day the bodies of the dead traitors were dragged from the room and thrown into an old abandoned well. The minstrel was placed in a rich coffin and buried with every honor in the church of Saint Augustine. On his headstone these words were inscribed: "Love and honor all minstrels in memory of this one." When mass had been sung, Leander had the traitors burned at the stake. He banished their families from his lands forever.

It was a month before Perceval's wounds were healed. He hoped for peace, but one day Leander told him their truce was at an end: "My blood still boils at the thought that you killed my father!" Ysmaine pleaded with her husband to forgive Perceval: "It is a sad thing when two noble knights fight each other, and you may be at a disadvantage because you refused his offer to make amends."

Leander knew this was good advice but had no intention of following it. All the brothers were once again intent on revenge. Leander armed himself and mounted. Perceval did the same. Everyone rushed out to see the battle. The lines were carefully drawn so that neither knight would have the sun in his eyes. Leander shouted his challenge to Perceval, and instantly they spurred their horses and charged, striking each other so hard they both fell to the ground. They fought on with their swords, so hard and so well that no one could tell who was winning, but suddenly Leander was flat on the ground, with Perceval's sword at his throat! Leander knew he was finished, unless he begged for mercy. He wondered what his father would want him to do, but it seemed he would be of little use to anyone if he were dead. He clasped his hands together and asked Perceval to spare him: "I have been your enemy, but now I promise to be your loyal friend."

"Will you and your brothers forgive me?"

"Yes, I swear it."

"No!" shouted Evander. "You will have to fight me first!"

Leander's wife fell to her knees and pleaded with Evander not to cause his brother's death. Marmadus intervened; he would rather be hanged than forgive Perceval! Meliadus, however, thought it sad enough to have lost their father. "Why must we lose our brother too? I'd rather have my heart ripped out! And Leander is the best fighter in the country! What makes you think you'd win? We would do ourselves more honor by making peace."

Finally, Meliadus convinced them. The brothers went to Perceval, still holding his sword to Leander's throat, and said, "My lord, we beg you to have mercy on our brother. We will make peace with you, release all our prisoners, and from now on consider you our good friend."

"If you will swear to that, I agree."

They swore by all they held dear. Then Perceval and the brothers disarmed and embraced each other.

When the great doors of the prison were unbarred, the captives trembled with fear, sure they were about to be led to their deaths. Only Gawain confronted his fate boldly. Perceval assured him that no one was to die and told him how he had come there and opened the casket, and the brothers had recognized their father inside, "the knight I killed with my javelin!"

The brothers had the Red Knight carried to the Church of Saint Brendan, where he was buried with great ceremony. Then they returned to the castle, where an elaborate meal had been prepared. Perceval sat next to Gawain at the high table, with the four brothers. They urged the knights to remain at the castle, at least for a while, but Gawain said he was going to Montesclaire to rescue the maiden. Leander thought another knight had already accomplished that feat, but he didn't know who it was. Perceval blushed and kept silent, not wanting to boast about his triumph over the knight whose shield bore a flame-throwing dragon. He simply said that he too must be on his way. The brothers accompanied them to a crossroads. Gawain turned left, toward Montesclaire. Leander said the middle road, toward Brittany, was the safest, but Perceval took the road to the right, from which no knight had ever returned.

*   *   *

AGAIN HE FOUND HIMSELF, as so often before, riding alone through the forest, following barely visible paths which led him deeper into a wilderness where now he found neither lodging nor adventure. His horse, weak from hunger, would surely die very soon, and he himself could not last much longer. He wondered if this was to be the end of his quest. But surely God would not leave him here to die all alone, with his task unfinished!

Just as his strength began to fail him, a violent storm arose, the rain coming down so hard it seemed to be bursting out of the ground, while hailstones pelted the earth from the dark sky. The roar of thunder was deafening, as bolts of lightning split the air and filled the forest with an unearthly light. Terrified by the noise, whipped by the wildly thrashing trees, Perceval's horse galloped frantically wherever he found a way, while the knight took what shelter he could from his shield. Thus he was borne along blindly for what seemed an eternity, and then, suddenly, all was still, and the moon came out from behind the clouds. Perceval rode on, grateful to be alive. In the distance he saw a little chapel, faintly lighted. It seemed to him miraculous to find a sign of human habitation, and he did not fail to thank God. As he rode in that direction, a few stars appeared in the sky, but by the time he dismounted and tethered his horse, the clouds had gathered again, and it was raining hard.

The chapel was unlocked. It was very cold inside, but Perceval was glad for any shelter. Exhausted, he pushed the door closed against the storm. A single candle glowed on the altar. Suddenly he knew where he was, and that he would find a dead knight lying there. Then the black fingers reached out and extinguished the light.

Standing there in the silent, tomb-like darkness, Perceval scarcely breathed as he waited for what must come. For long moments, nothing happened. Then, in the space of a lightning flash, he threw his lance at the hand, which caught it in midair and crushed it. The wall of the chapel cracked open, revealing a demon wrapped in fire. Perceval raised his shield as the apparition moved toward him. The air was thick with flames. Roof beams began to smoulder above his head, yet Perceval dared to attack. The point of his sword went straight to the monster's chest, but the blade bounced off as if it had struck rock and flew out of his hand. From deep within the fires that whirled around him, a terrifying voice roared, "Now you shall lie on the altar like the others!" Bereft of all defenses, Perceval grasped the hilt of the Fisher King's sword. He drew it from the scabbard, and the blade, which had broken so long ago, emerged intact! Its shining steel gleamed with a brilliant light, driving back the flames. With an ear-splitting shriek, the demon fled into the night, and Perceval fell unconscious to the stone floor.

An elderly priest was kneeling beside him when he awoke. The chapel was just as he had found it, with the candle once again alight on the altar. Together they approached the body of the knight, now burned beyond recognition. They carried him to a cemetery nearby where the priest said mass and the body was solemnly laid to rest. Countless shields hung from the branches of the trees; these belonged to knights the Black Hand had slain. But now the devil's dominion over the chapel was lost forever.

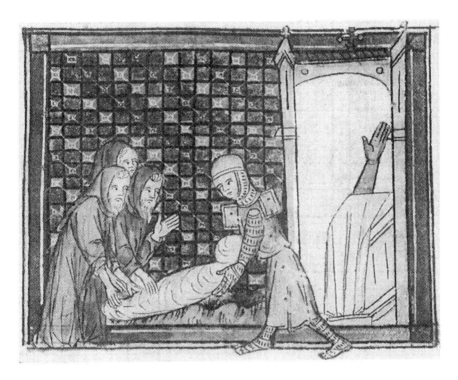

＊　　＊　　＊

IT SEEMED THE WHOLE FOREST had been refreshed by the storm when Perceval rode away the next morning. Water drops were sparkling in the sunlight, and birds were singing everywhere; he thought it had been a long time since he had heard their sweet music. Feeling at peace with the world, he gave his horse free rein, and soon they had left the forest behind. Beyond were farmlands where peasants were planting wheat, and orchards, their leaves almost hidden by flowers. A ferryman waited for him on the edge of a wide river. The Grail Castle appeared on the other side.

As servants hurried to help him dismount and lead his horse to the stables, the Fisher King came himself to welcome the knight. He strode firmly through the courtyard and embraced his nephew warmly. Perceval, overjoyed to see him in such good health, exclaimed, "How glad I am to see you well again, Uncle!"

"My wound was healed with the mending of your sword. It broke when you tried to force your way into a holy place, yet the rage which caused you to set its steel against stone was the pure rage of a child, denied what it longs for. I gave you the sword, perceiving in you the innocence that would draw you toward the wonder of the grail. And so it did, but your ambition to become a perfect knight prevented you from acting according to your nature. Your journey has been longer and harder than I imagined, but you have done much good in the world and have learned the truth of knighthood. Weapons have served you well against human evil, but against its very source you could do nothing. Yet you stood and confronted that power and knew that you possessed a power greater still."

Perceval was deeply moved by these words. The Fisher King embraced him, and together they walked to the great hall. The knight was surprised to hear sounds of festivity in a place which had always been silent. A noble company of lords and ladies greeted him there, acclaiming him their savior. These were the vassals of the Fisher King, gathered to rejoice in the lifting of the blight. The Fisher King led Perceval to the high table. When everyone was seated, the grail procession passed through the hall, filling the air with its radiant, golden light. There were tears of joy in Perceval's eyes as he once again saw the grail, the lance, and the silver carving dish. The grail and the lance went their way, but the silver dish, as before, reappeared in the hall, and the venison they were served was carved on it. It occurred to Perceval that nothing had ever been said about the carving dish, and he asked his uncle what its presence meant.

"The grail," said the Fisher King, "provides spiritual food, and the carving dish the nourishment of ordinary life, which is holy too."

In the evening, the Fisher King said that his father had requested Perceval's presence. The old king looked as fragile as an autumn leaf, but his voice was deep and resonant. He told how, when his son had come of age, he had given to him all power in the kingdom, having long wished to devote himself to spiritual things. When the land was overcome by evil forces, he had felt that the only way he could help would be to spend his life in prayer. His only sustenance came from the grail, which also brought him hope of the Fisher King's redemption. "That hope has been realized. The wasteland is no more, and I can at last end my vigil. Yet I did not want to die before I told you this: the holy symbols of the grail will leave the world when I do. But you, who have the gift of understanding, will keep them holy in the actions of your life. You have been greatly blessed, and you are a blessing to others. This is why I ask you to see that, when I die, I am buried in the chapel of Beaurepaire."

Perceval, overcome with emotion, knelt before the old king, thanking him and promising that his wishes would be carried out when the time had come. As the old king raised his hand in blessing, his head fell back against his chair. Perceval looked up and saw that he was dead. For a long time the knight did not move, as, with his whole being, he remembered the old king's words. Then he went into the great hall and told of that peaceful death which his listeners realized had nothing of sorrow in it.

The Fisher King and Perceval stayed with the old king all night. In the morning, the vassals were asked to assemble. The Fisher King told them that he would do as his father had done and devote his remaining years to prayer. He would retire to a monastery, leaving all his lands to Perceval. The knight who had saved them from the consequences of his sinful deed surely had the best claim to be their lord. He himself, striving to heal his soul and draw close to God, would not have to worry about the future of his kingdom. Then each one of the vassals came to kneel before Perceval and swear the oath of fealty, with his hands between his new lord's hands.

The old king's body was wrapped in a samite shroud and reverently placed in a rich casket. Then the funeral cortege set out for Beaurepaire, with Perceval going ahead to announce its coming. The countryside was familiar and welcoming; he knew the direction of Beaurepaire as a magnet knows the north. When he reached the top of a hill, he looked back toward Corbenic. The morning mists, drifting in a light breeze, blurred the outlines of the castle, which appeared and disappeared, insubstantial as a vision in a dream.

The sentry in the watchtower saw Perceval coming and blew his horn as a signal that the lord of the land had returned. Blanchefleur was in the courtyard even before he arrived, and he leaped off his horse and took her

in his arms. In the overwhelming joy of the moment, he forgot kings and kingdoms, wanting only to reassure her that he would not leave again. But there was much to be done before their many guests would arrive. Servants were set to work spreading freshly cut rushes over the floors, making sure the beds were ready, and preparing food. In the chapel, a marble slab near the altar was removed and a grave dug below it. By the time a suitable inscription had been engraved on the stone, the procession was already crossing the bridge. Perceval and Blanchefleur welcomed everyone and led them to the chapel, where a priest said mass. Then the body of the old king was gently placed in its grave.

The Fisher King said good-bye to Perceval the next morning, both of them saddened by the thought that they were unlikely to see each other again in this life. His former vassals stayed a little longer, and each expressed his gratitude to Perceval for having lifted the shadow from their lands. With mutual assurances of help in case of need and friendship at all times, they rode away, and Perceval and Blanchefleur were alone together at last.

Their years of separation had only added to their love. Perceval had felt that love was a temptation, a turning away from his quest, and Blanchefleur had tried to content herself with the hope that one day he would return. Now, completely untroubled, and certain that their union was sanctified by God, they gave themselves joyfully to their desire.

In the months that followed, it seemed that the perfection of their love illuminated all of Perceval's kingdom. Beaurepaire and Corbenic were united by the benevolent force of his presence. The peace he had known as a child in the uninhabited forest was protected in his lands by knights whose one ambition was loyal service. Blanchefleur watched over their people, making sure that no one suffered for lack of food or shelter. If anything caused them sorrow, they had at least the comfort of her concern. The ivory kegs that Perceval had wrested from the old hag were now empty, but their mere presence, it seemed, exerted a healing power over the land.

Early in the spring, Blanchefleur gave birth to their child, a daughter, as had been foretold. Wanting his friends and vassals to share his joy, Perceval sent messengers in all directions. By the time of the baby's christening, a multitude of distinguished lords and ladies had gathered in Beaurepaire. King Arthur, who had come with many of his knights, would be the child's godfather in memory of the long ago alliance between his father, Uther Pendragon, and Perceval's father. Blanchefleur, her health completely restored, was accompanied to the church by Guenevere and Perceval. After the ceremony, they all went in procession to the great hall where a feast had been prepared. When everyone was seated, servants appeared with gold and silver platters piled high with delectable foods.

Suddenly, all conversation ceased, and everyone was motionless, as if frozen in place. A brightness filled the hall, like the light of a thousand candles, and with it a music, soft and clear, whose sweetness drew tears from the eyes. Whether it came from instruments or from voices no one could tell. It floated through the air, more like a fragrance than a sound, and took the minds of the listeners into itself. Nothing existed but the joy that is eternal. Then the servers were moving through the hall, and the feast resumed. Perceval went on attending to his guests; the moment had passed for him as well. But he alone knew that music as something remembered, that light as a promise realized. The door in the stone wall had opened at last.

AFTERWORD

The following editions were used in the preparation of this version:

William Roach, ed. *Chrétien de Troyes: Le Roman de Perceval ou le Conte du graal* (Geneva: Droz, 1956).

William Roach, ed. *Continuations of the Perceval,* vols. 4 and 5 (Philadelphia: American Philosophical Society, 1971 and 1983).

Mary Williams, ed. *Gerbert de Montreuil: La Continuation de Perceval,* vols. 1 and 2 (Paris: Champion, 1922 and 1925).

Marguerite Oswald, ed. *Gerbert de Montreuil: La Continuation de Perceval,* vol. 3 (Paris: Champion, 1975).

A NOTE ON THE SOURCES

Chrétien's unfinished story of the grail quest was enormously popular in the late twelfth and early thirteenth centuries; it inspired at least four voluminous verse continuations dating from approximately 1200 to 1230.[1] Together these stories amount to some 60,000 lines; the length of the continuations and the disparate approaches of the continuators make a complete translation both undesirable and impractical.[2] In order to create a version of the grail legend that would be of manageable length and representative of the thirteenth-century tradition, we have had to make a number of choices.

Chrétien's *Story of the Grail,* unlike his other romances, is almost evenly divided between the adventures of two protagonists: the young and naive Perceval and the accomplished and worldly Gawain. The exact relation between the two parts of the story has long perplexed readers. Some scholars have argued that the two stories in effect "gloss" each other, exploring and expanding common themes and motifs; others have upheld the independence of the two segments, even suggesting that they were originally two different works, later "pasted" together by a scribe.[3] In our version, we have chosen to focus on Perceval, whose story comprises the first half of Chrétien's romance and who is accorded the privilege of witnessing the grail procession at the castle of the Fisher King. It is this vision — and the young knight's failure to ask the needed question — that sets him on a course of adventure and self-discovery.

Gawain, too, embarks on a quest in Chrétien's story: in the course of an ill-advised love affair, he is required to search for the bleeding lance, one of the three objects carried in the grail procession. Thus, in *The Story of the Grail,* Chrétien seems to be relating two parallel journeys to the Grail Castle, but the surviving text does not clarify the relation between them. We do know, however, that Gawain played a secondary role in three of Chrétien's earlier romances and his function in these was primarily to set off the achievements of the protagonist. It is also true that Gawain is consistently portrayed in Chrétien's earlier romances as an accomplished knight whose character is fixed; he does not grow or evolve. Perceval, by contrast, has everything to learn. His initial encounter with knights shows him to be by nature a seeker of knowledge, but lacking in both discernment and compassion. His later experiences lead him to the hard-won acquisition of both. Although Chrétien's intentions will never be known, it seems more than likely that Perceval, rather than Gawain, would be the one to achieve the quest, and for this reason we have preferred to base our version on episodes in which Perceval is the central figure.

Gawain, however, is an embodiment of knightly courtesy and charm, and the four thirteenth-century continuators of Chrétien's story were reluctant to bring his adventures to a conclusion. The so-called First Continuation, a 15,320-line work that takes up the story where Chrétien left it, is exclusively concerned with Gawain and ends with his unsuccessful visit to the Grail Castle. The Second Continuation, by "Wauchier" (otherwise unknown), is primarily concerned with Perceval but is centered around his search for a white stag at the behest of a mysterious maiden. In two manuscripts, the Second Continuation is followed by an extraordinary 18,000-line narrative attributed to the early-thirteenth-century writer Gerbert de Montreuil.[4] Gerbert differs from the other continuators in the attention he gives to unresolved episodes begun in Chrétien's narrative, but also because he is a brilliant writer, unknown even to many specialists.[5] As our list of sources shows, we have drawn the majority of episodes from the work of Gerbert.

Unfortunately, Gerbert, like the authors of the First and Second Continuations, and like Chrétien, seems to have left his version unfinished. A fourth continuation, generally known by the name of its author, "Manessier," does provide a conclusion to the grail story, but the author's heavy-handed religious symbolism is incompatible with the delicate balance Chrétien achieves between Christian beliefs and Celtic magic. In Manessier's conclusion, Perceval, having sworn to give up violence, is made to carry out an act of brutal vengeance at the request of the Fisher King. This is entirely foreign to the spirit of both Chrétien and Gerbert.

In Chrétien's romance, it is Perceval's mother who introduces the theme of the destructiveness of combat, and it is in regard to her that the need for compassion is first made apparent. The various wise men encountered by

Perceval, beginning with Gornemant, either emphasize compassion as a corrective to violence or, particularly in Gerbert's continuation, condemn violence as offensive to God. In keeping with the spirit of these authors, we have rewritten Manessier's story of the Fisher King's revenge. In our version, the king himself, rather than Perceval, kills Partinal and in so doing incurs the mysterious wound that never heals. His act, as he explains, is the cause of the devastation of his kingdom, the wasteland caused by the presence of the Black Hand, the ultimate manifestation of violence.

The emphasis on compassion in Chrétien and Gerbert has inclined us toward an interpretation of the grail procession that owes much to Per Nykrog. For Nykrog, the lance from whose tip a drop of blood continuously flows represents the violence of warriors: "Knights are by definition those who shed blood and who threaten to unleash horror and suffering until the king can rule his lands in peace."[6] As Nykrog points out, when Perceval leaves the Grail Castle he is immediately confronted with the violent aspect of knighthood. The subject is a familiar one in Chrétien's other works; we have only to think of the culminating scene in *Erec and Enide*, in which the hero releases an ordinary knight from the curse of spending his days in meaningless killing.

The other element in Chrétien's grail procession, the silver carving dish, is trivialized in Manessier's version, and dropped altogether in the other continuations, where it is replaced by a sword. Chrétien's symbols, however, were always carefully chosen; we have, therefore, restored the carving dish to its original prominence. In Chrétien's version, the carving dish brings real food which is served, in refined style, to ordinary human beings. The grail, in contrast, carries a single holy wafer, spiritual food which is the sole sustenance of the old king. The carving dish, it would seem, serves as a balance to the grail, confirming the spiritual value of secular life.

Chrétien's earlier works are marked by a joy in the terrestrial; in particular, they celebrate the happiness of human love. It therefore seems likely that the author would not have forgotten Perceval's promise to Blanchefleur but would have reunited the lovers, allowing the success of Perceval's quest to manifest itself within the context of human happiness.

Our version of this medieval legend owes much to the example of Joseph Bédier, who, one hundred years ago, created from the various fragmentary Tristan texts a complete and moving story.[7] We, too, have sought to bring new life to a great legend by making available to modern readers episodes that were well known in the Middle Ages but are unfamiliar today.

NOTES

1. These are the texts that can be properly referred to as "continuations" because they literally continue Chrétien's text. For a listing of the manuscripts, see Keith Busby et al., *The Manuscripts of Chrétien de Troyes* (Amsterdam: Rodopi, 1993), 14–15.

   Other thirteenth-century versions of the grail story include the verse *Roman de l'Estoire dou Graal* by Robert de Boron, where the grail is a chalice in which Joseph of Arimathea collects the blood of the crucified Christ; the prose Didot-*Perceval*, which is probably derived from both Robert de Boron's version and Chrétien's; the prose *Perlesvaus*, which relates the triple quest of Perceval, Gawain, and Lancelot; *La Queste del saint graal*, part of the vast prose work known as the Vulgate Cycle, in which the pure knight Galahad is introduced as the grail hero; and the great German poet Wolfram von Eschenbach's enormous *Parzifal*.

2. See, however, Nigel Bryant's *Perceval, The Story of the Grail* (Cambridge: D. S. Brewer, 1982; reprint 1996), in which the translator has included Chrétien's *Perceval* in its entirety along with generous selections from all four continuations. There is, of course, no attempt to create a coherent story from the various sources.

3. Among recent critics, Matilda Tomaryn Bruckner has argued persuasively for the former approach; see her "Rewriting Chrétien's *Conte du graal*—Mothers and Sons: Questions, Contradictions, and Connections," in *The Medieval Opus: Imitation, Rewriting, and Transmission in the French Tradition,* ed. Douglas Kelly (Amsterdam: Rodopi, 1996), 213–44, and "The Poetics of Continuation in Medieval French Romance: From Chrétien's *Conte du Graal* to the *Perceval* Continuations" (*French Forum* 18.2 [1993]: 133–49). In favor of the second approach, it is perhaps worth noting that the 1999 French Aggrégation examination focused exclusively on the Perceval portion of the story, indicating a current tendency to view the two stories independently of one another.

4. Another work, *Le Roman de la Violette*, is attributed to this same Gerbert. Nancy Vine Durling is currently preparing an English translation.

5. Sarah Sturm-Maddox is one of the few scholars to study the relation between Gerbert's continuation and Chrétien's romance. See her "'Tout est par senefiance': Gerbert's *Perceval*," in *The Arthurian Yearbook II* (New York: Garland Publishing, 1992), 191–207.

6. *Chrétien de Troyes, Romancier discutable* (Geneva: Droz, 1996), 196; our translation.

7. Bédier's version of *Le Roman de Tristan et Iseut* (Paris: H. Piazza, 1900) was translated into English by Hilaire Belloc in 1945; additional episodes were subsequently added by Paul Rosenfeld. The most recent edition is *The Romance of Tristan and Iseut*, retold by Joseph Bédier; translated by Hilaire Belloc and Paul Rosenfeld (New York: Vintage Books, 1994).

Patricia Terry is retired professor of literature at Barnard College and at the University of California, San Diego. Her many translations of medieval literature include *The Honeysuckle and the Hazel Tree: Medieval Stories of Men and Women*, *Renard the Fox*, *Poems of the Elder Edda*, and *The Song of Roland*.

Nancy Vine Durling has taught French and comparative literature at the University of California, Santa Cruz, and at Florida Atlantic University. She is editor of *Jean Renart and the Art of Romance: Essays on Guillaume de Dole* (Gainesville: University Press of Florida, 1997) and co-translator, with Patricia Terry, of *The Romance of the Rose or Guillaume de Dole by Jean Renart*.